LYNCH MOB JUSTICE!

"String him up!"

"Hang him, hang him..."

The words were quickly taken up and became a chant. Fists rose, the indictment rang forth, scowls of hatred carved every face. Doc glanced at Abington. He was quivering with fear, the sweat bursting from his forehead, his eyes so huge they threatened to pop from their sockets. The sheriff raised his eyes to look at the noose above him. Sight of it sent him into a paroxysm of dread. He fought his gag, his bonds, his fear.

The noose passed over the lowest limb and, hanging straight down, was lowered so that it framed Abington's terror-stricken face.

The chanting persisted. The judge placed the noose around Abington's neck. A cheer went up, propelled by a loud burst of applause.

J.D. HARDIN

THUNDER MOUNTAIN
MASSACRE

BERKLEY BOOKS, NEW YORK

THUNDER MOUNTAIN MASSACRE

A Berkley Book/published by arrangement with
the author

PRINTING HISTORY
Berkley edition/May 1987

ISBN: 0-425-09784-6

A BERKLEY BOOK® TM757,375
Berkley Books are published by The Berkley Publishing Group,
200 Madison Avenue, New York, N.Y. 10016.
The name "BERKLEY" and the stylized "B" with design are trademarks
belonging to Berkley Publishing Corporation.

CHAPTER ONE

Raider sneezed loudly, wetly, firing germs unimpeded twelve feet in front of him over the heads of other passengers, awakening half the occupants of the car.

"Can't you cover your mouth?" asked Doc Weatherbee, his partner, sitting in the window seat beside him, and one of those jolted out of his dreams.

"It slipped out. I got a bad cold, fierce; probably pneumonia."

"Whatever you've got there's no reason to give it to the rest of humanity. Put your hand over your mouth and go back to sleep."

Doc provided an example, going back into his slouch against the window post, tilting his curly-brim derby down over his face and refolding his arms. A quarter moon slid across the sky, the stars glimmered tiredly, the bleak uninspired landscape of northern Nevada moved past, interrupted briefly as they rolled over the bridge spanning Rock Creek. In the distance the black eminence of Haystack Peak rose into the cobalt sky.

1

"I can't sleep," groused Raider, shifting his weight and snuffling disgustingly. Heads turned, sleepy eyes glared, faces expressed disapproval and disdain. "I got a bad cold," he announced. No one said a word. "It gets worse at night; my brisket's all filled up with phle-gum." No one cared. The faces turned away, the chorus of snoring resumed. "I ache all over. I should be in bed, that's what I should. If I haven't got pneumonia already I'll sure as hell get it sittin' up in a drafty damn cattle car 'steada layin' in a warm bed."

"Shut up!" demanded a voice six seats forward.

"Shut up yourself."

The train creaked and groaned and jolted over the ties. Rock Creek was well behind them, Haystack Peak fled from sight, only the moon kept pace. Raider emulated his partner, tilting his hat down, slouching and folding his arms, but sleep would not come. He was preparing to wake Doc and tell him so and remind him how bad his cold was when the train began to slow. Seconds later it stopped altogether, so abruptly everyone in the car was jolted awake. Doc's derby fell from his face, bounced off one knee, and landed on the floor.

A rifle cracked. Two more shots followed. As one the passengers ducked, save for Raider and Doc who sat bolt upright.

"Jesus Christ," groused Raider. "Middle o' the goddamn night, high-line riders come to call, and me with a cold. This is all we need."

Doc was on his feet, shoving one leg against Raider's. "Move. Back to the express car. Maybe we can help."

Raider grunted, mumbled protest, and cursed under his breath, but he got to his feet and started toward the rear. Doc brushed by him, his nickel-plated .38 Diamondback gleaming in his hand. They hurried toward the end door, Doc continuing on through into the car behind while Raider sneaked a look out the open vestibule window. Three riders in dusters with bandannas over their faces were milling about, firing in the air, getting the show started. Others crouched behind an outcropping on the other side of the siding paralleling the main line. As Raider spotted them they opened up, splitting the night with a withering fusillade directed the sliding side door of the express car one behind the car Doc had just entered. By the time both Pinkertons got through the car, elbowing their way down the aisle clogged with rudely awakened, hysterical, furious, and confused passengers and into the express car, the attackers were pouring everything they had at it.

A lone messenger defended the car, but a formidable-looking defender he was, standing at least six foot four in his shirtsleeves with sleeve garters, gauntleted sorting gloves, and green-visored cap, and weighing in the neighborhood of an eighth of a ton, all muscle and grit. He was down on one knee, his seven-shot Spencer thrust through a knothole, one eye pressed against a slit between the boards, pouring lead at the outlaws.

"We're Pinkertons," boomed Doc above the din. "I'm Weatherbee, he's Raider."

"Aaron Cobble. Welcome aboard."

Raider yawned, swiped his eyes with the back of his hand, examined the side, found a knothole, and knelt and checked his .45, spinning the cylinder. Then he sneezed moistly.

"I won't be much good, Aaron Cobble. I got a devil of a cold. Can't breath; can't swallow hardly; can't hardly see, my eyes are so full up with it. I'll do what I can, but—"

"Oh shut up, Rade," snapped Doc, positioned on the other side of the door.

The firing outside suddenly stopped. A voice called out, a gravelly whiskey baritone.

"You in there, give it up 'fore somebody gets hurt. We don't wanna kill nobody. Jest open the door and stand with your hands high and no tricks and we'll be in and out and gone 'fore you know it. Fair 'nough?"

Aaron fired three times. A man screamed, the speaker cursed, the barrage resumed. Over the next ten minutes nearly a hundred shots penetrated the side of the car, splintering wood from floor to ceiling, with most of the hits centered on the door.

"They can shoot at that door till Christmas, it won't do 'em a lick o' good," said Aaron. "There's a three-inch band o' steel reinforcement all the way round the edge, and an inch-thick plate round the lock. They'd need dynamite to blow it loose."

"Don't be surprised if they get round to tryin' just that. What the hell you carryin' they're so eager to get? Gold? Silver?"

"There's about four hundred in gold in the box—"

A rifle poked through a crack in the side door.

"Get 'em up in there."

Raider marched over and brought his right boot down full force on the barrel, smashing it free of the outlaw's grip, bending it useless where it joined the stock. A shot found its way inside, bouncing harmlessly off his shoulder.

"Asshole," he muttered.

Passengers along the full length of the train were beginning to return the fire directed at the express car, attracting some of the attackers' attention. Firing at the express car became sporadic. The battle kept up for two hours, with neither side getting the upper hand. Doc was hit twice—first a flesh wound in the leg, then a slug grazed his left cheek, skinning it slightly. Aaron was hit in the shoulder, but gamely shook it off and continued firing his aged Spencer, heating the barrel so he yelled when he inadvertently grabbed it. Raider sneezed and fired, sneezed and fired, moving from slit to slit. He claimed three hits.

"Tell us when you get to ten," Doc advised. "There's got to be at least thirty out there."

No sooner had he spoken than the locomotive whistled, began chuffing loudly, and came puffing backwards down the siding, passing the express car.

"What the hell . . ." began Raider.

"Brace yourselves, boys," warned Aaron. "They're gettin' ready to ram us from behind."

"What for?" asked Raider.

"I'm getting the distinct impression that they want in here," said Doc dryly.

The battle continued. In between shots at the rear end of the car they could hear the mail car, the last car in the string, being uncoupled and rolled away— to be used as a battering ram. All three stiffened, waiting. Tense moments later it was slammed into the express car so hard it nearly derailed it.

"Tol'ja!" boomed Aaron. "Crazy idjits!"

Three more times the mail car, hooked to the cowcatcher of the engine, was backed up, the throttle lever thrown, and the engine bulled forward, smashing the mail car into the express car, all but upending the occupants and sending sacks and boxes bouncing about like peas in a bucket. The ramming was irritating and unnerving, but failed in its obvious purpose: to crush the rear of the express car and spring open the side door.

"Stupid jackasses!" burst Aaron. "If they only knew..."

"What?" Doc asked.

"There's a half million in silver in the mail car. From the Washoe diggings. They got themselves a silver batterin' ram and don't even know it. Stupid, stupid!"

After the fourth failure the outlaws gave it up. The firing stopped again. The leader repeated his threat offer; when Raider rejected it with some colorful allusions to him and his parents the shooting resumed. Then over the din rose the strident whistle of an eastbound train.

"That's number seven heading for Elko, Deeth, and Wetts," announced Aaron.

They held their fire, as did the attackers, as number seven rumbled along the siding. But when it had cleared the battlefield, it stopped.

"Oh boy," muttered Raider.

"Now they got two trains," said Aaron. "They're bitin' off more'n they can chew for fair."

As if realizing the wisdom of this observation and agreeing, the leader bellowed an order.

"Get yourselves the hell outta here pronto!"

Away rolled number seven.

"Keeping it's dumb," said Aaron. "Lettin' it go is even dumber." He chuckled. "That train'll be in Beowawe in a hour. The conductor'll give the alarm and they'll send out a posse."

"An hour," groused Raider. "'It'll be two, maybe more by the time they get here."

"It's a Mexican standoff up to now," said Doc. "It could go on like this until noon. In which case—"

Scuffling sounded directly over their heads. Raider emptied his gun into the ceiling. They stiffened and listened intently. All that could be heard was the sporadic firing coming from outside. Then chopping. The blade of an ax showed. Raider had reloaded; he fired. The slug clanged off the blade, ricocheted against the side of the safe, and bounced harmlessly on the floor.

"Will you be careful!" boomed Doc. "You'll kill somebody."

Before Raider could respond the side door blew, the explosion clanging painfully against their eardrums, sending needles of pain into their brains; all three were tossed head over heels. Raider landed, banging his shoulder against the rear wall, yelling and swearing. Smoke billowed inward, bringing the acrid stench of cordite. All three had lost their weapons. Into the car poured the attackers.

The one who had been shouting orders ordered them to reach. He looked even older than the picture his voice had printed on Doc's mind, a grizzled and gnarled stump of a man, his bones haphazardly assembled in the sack of his skin; he carried a rancid stink in with him, testimony to his disdain for soap and water. He was toothless, he was ugly, his eyes were watery and shining with triumph, his breath was as foul as his body odor. Lord of the moment, he waved two .44s, his holsters slipping along his belt and meeting at his crotch above his bowlegs.

As his three companions held the Pinkertons and Aaron

at bay, their hands high, the man stepped forward. "I oughta kill you bastards where you stand!"

Raider sneezed.

"Shut up!"

"I sneezed. I got a cold. Pneumonia."

"Shut up, I said."

He flipped his gun, grabbed the barrel, and knocked Raider cold. Doc gasped, as did Aaron. They were the last sounds from either; down went one then the other, similarly dispatched.

"Shove the rest o' the dyne under the safe, Jace. We'll blow it through the roof and these boys with it."

CHAPTER TWO

The spike driver's upper body made the village black-
smith's look puny by comparison. He was John Henry's
big brother, and he wielded the twelve-pound sledge as
effortlessly as a flyswatter. Up it went, poised a second,
and down it came, smashing the spike dead on. Only it
wasn't a spike, it was a human head, and attached to it was
Raider's face. With each blow he grimaced in pain; it shattered his skull, flared through his head, mashed his brain.

He woke. Slivers of daylight shone through the cracks.
When he turned his head there was a huge square picture of
Nevada, the frame out of which the door had been blown.
The safe looked as if it had been dropped on concrete from
a mile's height: the door hung from its upper hinge; papers
and compartments were strewn about the floor.

Aaron Cobble groaned. Raider watched his massive
hand steal to his head and find the bump; he flinched and
groaned again. Doc sat up gingerly, inspecting his forehead. A bump the size of a hen's age showed. Voices could
be heard outside. Riders were milling about. Somebody

8

shouted. Raider winced and cursed. Again a shout.

"Will you shut the hell up out there! Ahhhhhhh . . ."

His own voice actuated more severe pain.

"Did you see that mangy son of a bitch cold-cock me? He fractured my skull. Feel there, Doc, tell me it isn't fractured." He sneezed. "Owwww! Hittin' a sick, helpless man. I find that bastard I'll hammer him with his gun butt so flat they'll be able to roll him up like a damn sleepin' bag!"

"You all right, Aaron?" Doc asked solicitously.

"Will be. That the posse outside?"

"I think so. And our friends are long gone, I'm sure. Why else would the posse be hanging around?"

Two men wearing badges climbed in over the wreckage of the door. One was in his sixties, old but rugged-looking, slim-waisted, hard-muscled, and handsome, with silver-gray hair and a matching flowing mustache. The other was half his years and looked sickly; he was round-shouldered, with a consumptive chest and an expression on his homely face that suggested his stomach was giving him trouble. He was chewing tobacco. He spat at the safe. Doc's stomach rumbled and he turned from the sight.

"You boys okay?" asked the older man.

"Great," said Raider. "Don't we look it?"

"You're alive, which is more than can be said for five of theirs, three of your fellow passengers, and the engineer. They put eleven bullets in his chest."

"He musta mouthed off," said Raider.

"I'm Marshal Tutweiler, Beowawe."

He extended his hand to Raider, who, busy reinspecting his bump, waved acknowledgment. Doc introduced them and filled the marshal in on the holdup.

"We got here about ten minutes ago. By that time they were well away. We talked to some of the passengers. The consensus of opinion says they rode north toward the Idaho border. We're getting ready to ride out. You boys want to come along?"

Doc frowned. "If they're well away, as you say, what would be the use?"

"Maybe they don't know the posse come," said Aaron. "Maybe once outta sight they're slowin' down, doggin' it."

"They'd be stupid to," said Doc.

"They didn't seem overly bright," said Raider. "Might at least be worth a shot. Whatta ya say, Doc?"

"I guess."

"Have you got horses?" asked the marshal.

"In the mail car," said Raider, "if they didn't get bounced to death in the rammin'."

"Get them. Make it fast."

Raider and Doc went out with his companion.

The marshal bent and examined Aaron's bump. "A beauty. They tell me you three put up quite a fight before they blew in the door. What was in the safe?"

"Four hundred in gold; about a hundred and fifty in paper; letters, contracts, the usual. Nothing that can't be duplicated." Aaron glanced about. "What a mess." He sifted through the papers strewn in front of the safe. "Gold and the money are gone; they left the rest. They left half a million in silver in the mail car."

"Do tell. We checked it; they didn't get into it. This appears to be your lucky day, son."

"Yeah."

Raider and Doc rode on either side of Marshal Tutweiler. There were thirteen men in all; four deputies and six speedily deputized volunteers had accompanied him from Beowawe. Thunder Mountain rose to their left. Ahead stretched the Tuscaroras, and beyond, the Owyhee River twisted its way into its South Fork.

The Idaho border was nearly a hundred miles distant, through mountainous country sparsely studded with vegetation. Intersecting the mountains were numerous ravines and passes, so that the route was fairly direct. Bunch grass, creosote bushes, greasewood, and sagebrush abounded, but the lack of rain lent every growing thing a withered look.

Marshal Tutweiler was a talker. He seemed fascinated with the Pinkertons, questioning Doc at great length about the agency and their experiences in the field. Raider was not eager for conversation; he felt "god-awful," and sneezed his way north with monotonous regularity, his nose running like a broken tap, his eyes puffy, his head aching furiously. They reached the border in the middle of the afternoon. It was identified by a battered sign on which a grayish-brown, white-spotted sage thrush perched to welcome them. Tutweiler raised his arm, signaling a halt. Raider, Doc, and the others gathered around him.

"I didn't think we'd catch up with them," said the marshal, "but we had to try."

"You're not giving it up," said Doc.

"Read that sign. This is where Nevada ends and Idaho begins."

"Oh for Chrissakes," groused Raider.

"Sorry, boys, you're welcome to keep on after them."

"Thanks."

"We've got to head back. They're out of our jurisdiction; matter of fact, they were back there in Lander County where they held you up. We're Eureka County, this is Elko; has been for the last seventy miles."

"We can do without the geography lesson," said Raider.

"We understand," said Doc. "We'll keep going. We're obliged to. The Southern Pacific has a contract with the agency. It's up to us to at least try to catch them. We'll keep at it till we do."

Raider sneezed. "Or till I die, whichever comes first."

Doc ignored him, as did the others. "I do wish we had something to go on," he said. "When you talked to the passengers, did anyone by chance recognize any of them? Some of them did remove their bandannas when the shooting started."

Tutweiler thought a moment and shook his head. "Afraid nobody spotted any of them. Only thing they were sure of was that they took off dead north."

"That doesn't mean beans," said Raider. "They coulda

cut east, west, doubled back. By now they could be half-way to California."

Tutweiler smiled. "Is he always so bright and cheerful?" he asked Doc.

"Please, this is one of his better days."

"Awww." Raider waved away both. "I got pneumonia. I practically got one foot in the grave. Whatta ya want from me, a song an' dance, for Chrissakes? Go if you're goin', Marshal. Come on, Weatherbee."

Doc grabbed his reins. "Hold it, hold it."

"I just want to add one thing," said the marshal, "for what it's worth. It's quite a ways up, and it may not be where they're heading at all, but if I were to keep going I'd head for Silver City. It's at least another hundred miles, but they could very well be heading there. It's the only wide-open town for two hundred miles in every direction. They'd be safe there."

"Thanks for the tip," said Doc.

"Could be a wild goose chase," said Raider.

Tutweiler nodded. "It could be. I'm just tossing it in the hat for your consideration. If you do go on, make sure you check it out."

"Hey, Marshal."

A young fellow wearing bibs washed out bone-white and a Union Army cap had dismounted at the rear of the pack and was examining the ground.

"There's a flock o' tracks here, like a bunch stopped and ambled about before going' on."

"He's right," said another man. "They crossed right here by the sign."

"There's a start for you," said Tutweiler.

"Coulda been sixteen other guys," said Raider. "Hey, son, anybody scratch his name in the dust?"

"Let's go, Rade. Thanks again, Marshal."

"Good hunting."

He waved them off. They crossed into Idaho, following the flight of the sage thrush, picking up the Owyhee River dried to a trickle on their left.

They rode through Duck Valley into the Owyhee Mountains, picking up the tracks repeatedly—or at least the tracks of a large group of riders that Doc was resolutely certain belonged to their quarry.

"How many gangs have passed this way recently? And with it so dry, the wind would blow away any tracks more than a few hours old. Silver City sounds better and better. I wouldn't be surprised if we caught up with them before nightfall." Doc nodded in punctuation of his optimism.

"Why don't you wait till dark so's you can whistle in it? I mean, what is all this heapin' hope and horseshit up in a pile with the same shovel? What you doin', readin' tea leaves?"

"You can't wait to get your hands on Mr. Stink, isn't that so? You said you can't."

"What I want and what we'll get could be different as a buzzard and a bird dog and likely is. I'm sick, Doc."

"I know, you've told me."

"I need rest, a bed, a bottle o' whiskey, a honey and apple cider vinegar tonic. Nothin' chases a cold like honey and apple cider vinegar, you know. Sage tea's good too. My mother used to grease a cloth, spread it with ground lobelia herb, heat it, and lay it 'cross my chest and aroun' back 'cross my shoulders. Worked like a charm."

"Can you do anything with sagebrush, greasewood, or creosote? Because that's about all we've seen since the border."

"A bag o' asafetida worn round the neck works."

"Rade . . ."

"How about we stop off in the next town at a drugstore? I could get me some Scott's Emulsion; Hammonds Cold Pellets are good."

"That stuff is worthless, take it from me. Didn't I used to use a homeopathic medicine wagon for a cover? Besides, what 'next town'? We haven't seen two houses together for more than a hundred and eighty miles."

"Gotta come to a town sometime. We can't ride all the way to Canada."

They moved between bone-dry Boulder Creek on their left and the equally arid Castle Creek to the right. They had passed two arrow signs, one lying on the ground at the foot of its post, indicating Silver City dead ahead. To the right, angling north-northwest, stretched the Owyhee Range; on the opposite side ran the Snake River. Silver City, with neighboring DeLamar west of it, nestled in the shadow of the range. They had yet to spy it when they rounded an outcropping and into view came a sprawling ramshackle ranch house with a corral filled with horses.

"Oh boy," rasped Raider. "Full house. Must be thirty horses in that pen there."

He had pulled up. He shaded his eyes from the setting sun.

Doc came up alongside. "You think it's them?"

"How the hell am I s'posed to know? You think I can see through walls? Let's get back behind the rock."

They did so and none too soon. Men came filing out the back door.

"Looky there, it's Mr. Stink in the flesh. Look at those bowlegs, the raunchy-lookin' duds. Chrissakes, I can smell him from here." He felt the bump on his head. "Look at the son of a bitch, jauntier'n a Shanghai rooster."

"There's the one who came into the car with him, and the others. What a break!"

"Whatcha talkin' about, 'break'? We followed their tracks on and off, that marshal said Silver City, and it can't be more'n six miles further on. Their horses are still sweaty, they can'ta been here more'n a half hour or so. They just poked along and we caught up. It all fits, Doc."

"I thought you said it wouldn't, it was a wild goose chase."

"I never said that. You're hearin' things. Must be that bump on your brow."

"What'll we do?"

Raider accorded him a jaundiced look. "Whatta ya

wanta do, walk up and interduce ourselves? Leave 'em be for now. We know where they're campin'; I'll stick here and make sure they stay put. You ride around the other side to Silver City and buttonhole the sheriff. We're gonna need lotsa guns. Make sure you tell him Mr. Stink's got himself a army. Color it up some, like they killed fourteen women and children down to Thunder Mountain, maybe kidnapped a couple pretty little misses, killed their pappies in cold blood."

"I don't think that's necessary. They did enough damage to get him to stir his stumps. Leave it to me."

"Get goin'. And if you see a drugstore get me somethin' for my pneumonia, okay?"

Doc heeled his horse and dusted away.

Silver City, Idaho, was a far cry from the town of the same name in southwestern New Mexico, center of a metal-mining and stock-raising region and distinguished as the first town incorporated in New Mexico in 1878. Silver City, Idaho, was one main street, sun-baked in summer, rock-hard in winter, lined by false-fronted places of business, saloons, gambling establishments, and dance halls. With an eye to perpetuating the town, attracting business, and beautifying the street, merchants had erected board sidewalks. The sheriff's office, rendered conspicuous by the bulletin board out front crammed with wanted posters, was sandwiched between Hurtlemeyer's Cash Store and Kleck's Union Market.

Doc dismounted and hitched his weary mustang to the rail.

"Patience, little girl. I'll get you a bushel of sweet oats, all the water you can drink, and a nice brushing-down soon as I have a word with the sheriff."

As if responding to his arrival, a barrel-chested, clean-shaven man reeking of bay rum and sporting twin gold teeth in the upper center of his grin came out of the office. He turned his back on Doc to deliver a few final words to someone inside, then laughed uproariously. Turning to face his visitor, he began rolling a cigarette.

"Sheriff . . ."

Sheriff Nat Abington and he exchanged introductions. Up close, appraising the man, looking into his cold blue eyes, Doc got an uneasy feeling of mistrust. Abington seemed to have difficulty looking him straight in the eye as they talked. He also had a habit of interrupting before Doc could complete a sentence, and no sooner did he get into the reason for his visit then the sheriff began to act like he wanted to get away from him.

"They turned the place into a bloodbath, all for less than six hundred—"

"You contact the law down there?"

"They got a posse over as fast as they could, but by the time they got there . . ." He shrugged. "They rode with us to the border. We left them there. It was a matter of juris—"

"You say you and your sidekick are Pinkertons? Where's he at?"

"Watching their hideout."

"Where might that be?"

"About six miles southeast of town. Looks like an old stock ranch. I'll be frank—we'll need all the help we can get, at least twenty men with rifles. It might make sense to wait until dark."

Abington licked his paper and rolled his cigarette one last turn. He began fishing through his pockets. Doc produced a kitchen match, lit it with his thumb, and offered it. The sheriff lit up and sucked his lungs full.

"Dark, yeah."

"How many deputies do you have?"

"Four regulars. There's two others help out now and then. Sounds pretty dangerous, I mean with them bein' pros, heavily armed, killers. That Patchett place may not look all that sturdy, but old man Patchett built it solid as a fort back when. It's stood up through lotsa winds and knocked plenty o' barns down—houses, too."

"We need your help," Doc said evenly.

"I heard you the first time. Twenty men, you say. Never got up a posse that big in the six years I been sheriff here."

An attractive young couple passed them. The woman smiled at Doc, pointedly, he thought, ignoring the sheriff. Her escort nodded curtly to him.

"Am I to understand you're not interested?"

"Hold your horses now, did I say that? I didn't say that. I just said—"

"I heard. Thirty minutes should be ample time to round up a fair-sized crowd. At least twenty, better twice that. Why don't I come back in half—"

"Sure, you do that. I'll see you."

With this Abington turned about and walked back into the office. Doc stared at the closed door for a long moment. He could feel his cheeks warming as he began to seethe. The sheriff wasn't interested; he wanted no part of any posse; he had better things to do. Doc started off to his right after the young couple. Passing the window, he could see Abington sitting down to checkers with an older man. Doc hurried his step. He caught up with the passersby in front of Kincaide's Photograph Studio. He took off his hat and introduced himself. They were Joshua Kincaide and his wife Alvina. They made a handsome couple—well-dressed, well-spoken, well-bred. In sharp contrast to Sheriff Nat Abington.

"Would you think me forward if I asked you a few questions about the town? I just got here."

"Not at all," said Josh. "Come on in."

The studio was a single large square room with a drape in the rear behind which, Doc assumed, Josh developed his plates. Stairs to the right led to the second floor. Atop its tripod stood an Empire State camera with reversible back; two other cameras, a viewfinder, and a plate holder occupied a side table. A sylvan background displaying varied shades of green stood eight feet tall at the rear alongside the drape, and other backgrounds leaned against a wall, one atop another. Portraits of Silver City's residents graced the walls, with group shots of school classes, clubs, a church choir, well-armed innocents, soiled doves, and Sheriff Nat Abington grinning triumphantly and wielding an ivory-gripped six-shooter. Two light reflectors were directed at a stool set in front of the woodsy background, and to one side stood a section of rail fence with a coiled lariat slung over one post. Alvina excused herself to go upstairs and boil water for the tea.

"I won't beat about the bush," said Doc. He showed his Pinkerton I.D.

Josh was impressed. "You sure came to the right place," he said. "This town has more crime than Deadwood and Dodge City combined. Not more crime. What I mean is more criminals."

"I don't follow you."

"Silver City is where they come when they're on the run, mostly from Oregon and Nevada, being as they're so close. The Jameses, the Youngers, the Daltons, the Hole-in-the-Wall Gang—you name them, they've all hidden out here at one time or another."

"What about Sheriff Abington?"

Josh laughed lightly but bitterly. "Good old Nat, sworn to uphold the law, the badge, and the gun, protector of us all. The man's as larcenous as any of those he shields."

Footsteps. Alvina came down the stairs carrying a tray of sugar cookies, their delicious odor preceding their arrival.

"Joshua," she said reprovingly.

"He's not, Vinny? The man's the soul of corruption, and you know it."

His frankness embarrassed her. She flashed Doc an apologetic look, wincing slightly and forcing a weak smile. She left the tray and excused herself a second time to go back and see to the tea.

"Vinny doesn't like me to talk about Abington, but I wouldn't be able to look at myself in the mirror if I didn't tell you the truth about him. I take it you asked for his help in some matter."

Having identified himself, Doc could see no reason to

conceal why he'd come to town. Josh seemed to sink deeper and deeper into discouragement as he listened, as if he'd heard it all before and knew too well from experience the futility of trying to snatch somebody out from under the sheriff's protective wing.

"What does the leader look like?"

Doc described him. Josh rolled his eyes.

"You know him?"

"Not intimately, thank goodness, but I could hardly mistake your description. He's Ira Pickett, one of Abington's bosom buddies. He's been murdering and robbing, rustling and running for more than forty years. He and Nat go way back."

"Let me understand something. Abington being the law in this town, does he control everything and everybody?"

"Not directly. He's too clever for that. Let's say enough so that his hands-off policy is in no great danger of being revoked. There's the mayor and Judge Aldergate, both so old and wishy-washy they wouldn't dream of crossing him. There's no shortage of upright citizens, but they just turn a blind eye to his shenanigans. Why shouldn't they? The people he protects don't bother them. It's the old story: the decent element isn't organized; the indecent is very well organized."

"The guns are on Abington's side."

"Exactly. Ira Pickett and others like him cut him in on their ill-gotten gains in exchange for his protection. Against the likes of you. Conscientious peace officers come into this town not knowing the situation, looking for bad eggs, meet with fatal accidents with surprising regularity. The cemetery out back of Lassiter's Feed and Grain is filled with people like you. Mr. Weatherbee, my advice is to get out of here before dark."

"I plan to. I just have to see to my horse; we've come a long way. I appreciate your candor, Mr. Kincaide, and I'll get out, but I don't intend to stray too far. My partner and I came up here to collar Ira Pickett and his friends, and that's precisely what we're going to do."

"Don't say I didn't warn you."

Doc smiled. "I won't."

"You did tip your hand to Abington."

"Guilty." Doc sighed and shook his head. "Rash, impulsive me, I took it for granted the sheriff was upholding the law; it never occurred to me he'd be flaunting it. It appears my partner and I will have to get our help outside. I'll have to wire agency headquarters in Chicago. Where's the Western Union office?"

"There is no separate office, if that's what you mean. There's a clerk and a key and the file cabinet in the window of Hurtlemeyer's Cash Store."

"I see."

"Right next door to the sheriff's office."

"Oh dear."

"I know the clerk, Abel Townsend. If you want to send a message, give it to me and I'll see that Abel sends it out and on the q.t."

Doc tilted his face and studied Josh from underneath his upper lids. "You can trust me," said Josh.

"Of course." He laughed. "If I can't after all I've told you, I'm a dead man."

Alvina gasped. She had descended the stairs with the tea without either of them noticing her.

"What are you cooking up now, Joshua Kincaide?"

"Not a thing, love. I'm just going to send a telegram for Mr. Weatherbee here."

He got out a pad and pencil.

"Where's the nearest town with a railroad?" asked Doc.

Josh scratched his head and frowned.

"There's Caldwell up north on the far side of the mountains," said Alvina. "And Mountain Home to the east. They're both quite a ways."

"Our reinforcements'll probably come into Mountain Home. They can get horses there." Doc printed his message and the address and handed it to Josh. "I'm asking for twenty-four men; I'll be lucky to get half that. It depends on how many operatives we have in the area and how many of them can be freed from their assignments."

Doc tried to give Josh money, but he refused it.

"Please, consider it our contribution to Nat Abington's downfall. I only hope you can make it happen."

As Doc sipped he thought about Raider and his "pneumonia," and wished he might take some hot tea back with him. Halfway through his second cup and third cookie Josh inquired about his partner. Doc cited the many contrasts between them, he himself coming from Boston, Harvard-educated; Raider coming from a farm near Viola in Fulton County, Arkansas, leaving school at the ripe old age of ten, reaching adulthood bringing along "the finest, shrewdest, most perceptive mind" Doc had ever encountered and the "spleen and experience to go with it." He asked Alvina if she had anything she could spare for Raider's cold.

Twenty minutes later he left surfeited with tea and cookies and a half bottle of Dr. Bloom's Cold Eradicator. Alvina praised it to the skies; he himself put little stock in any such concoctions, but fully expected Raider to share her enthusiasm. At that, he mused, as he mounted his horse and pointed her toward the nearest livery stable, wasn't every patent medicine liberally laced with the universal cure-all, the potent, most magic ingredient, mind over matter?

Sheriff Abington emerged from his office as he started off. "Hey, where you goin'?"

Doc pretended he didn't hear.

Abington laughed loudly.

"I thought you and me had a meeting."

Doc cursed him loudly under his breath. Outlaws were bad enough; lawmen protecting outlaws, in effect becoming outlaws themselves, were far worse.

This one he wanted. This one he'd get.

"He who laughs last, Sheriff."

CHAPTER THREE

By the time Doc was able to return to where he'd left Raider watching the house, darkness had arrived and a chill wind had come up, moaning about the outcropping, flapping the brim of Raider's Stetson and prompting him to draw his blanket tightly about his shoulders. He sat shivering. Doc's news did little to lift his spirits.

"You sayin' the law in town is in cahoots with all owl-hoots? *All* of 'em?"

"I'm telling you what I was told, and I see no reason not to believe it. I've wired Chicago. Bill Wagner'll be sending help."

"Good. Great. How many? Two guys, three?"

"We'll know when they get here, Rade. Isn't asking for reinforcements always throwing the dice? Have you ever known it to be otherwise?"

"Did you tell him what we're up against? That there's maybe fifty of 'em, all armed to the teeth, cold-eyed killers every one?"

"Relax. Be patient. Hey, I almost forgot, I brought you a present."

"Shit."

"Medicine for your cold."

Raider brightened. "Give it here, quick."

Doc drew the bottle Alvina Kincaide had given him from his inside coat pocket. Raider sneezed, covering his nose with his thumb and index finger.

"Dr. Bloom's Cold Eradicator. Mrs. Kincaide swears by it."

He presented the bottle. Raider snatched it from him, but his hand was moistened from covering his sneeze; no sooner did he get hold of it than it slipped from his grasp, dropped straight down, and shattered on a rock.

"Oh for Chrissakes!"

"You clumsy oaf!"

"It's your fault. Don't you even know how to hand a body somethin'? You leggo before I could get a firm hold, you asshole. Jesus Christ, will you look at that."

"Clumsy."

"Shut up!"

"That's that. I'm sorry, Rade."

"You should be, goddamn it! Well, what are we gonna do, sit here all night freezin' our asses off? I'm hungry, I need a drink, and look at my horse. She's beat to hocks, poor girl."

Doc threw a glance at the house. Yellow light filled both side windows and the double window above the kitchen sink. The horses in the corral stood stock still. No sound could be heard inside the house. Raider, too, stared at it.

"Look at the bastards, all snug and warm, plenty o' hot eats, all the whiskey they can swallow, you bet." He sneezed wetly. "Come on, we're goin' into town and get us something to eat and a bottle and a bed. What the hell, they're not goin' anywheres. We can come back out in the mornin'."

"Okay, but not Silver City. I don't want to chance

bumping into the sheriff. Not this early in the game, at any rate."

"Get the map outta my saddlebag."

Doc did so. He spread it on the ground, avoiding the spot where the bottle had broken. He lit a match.

"DeLamar's the closest, see there? Just west of Silver City."

"Looks to be about seven miles."

"Know anything about it?"

"Never been there, but it can't be any worse than Silver City. Let's go."

DeLamar looked to be half the size and population of Silver City, but seemed to be spared the intruding riffraff. As with Sheriff Abington's stamping grounds, Indians added to the population. The southwest corner of Idaho was Shoshone country. The Shoshone were originally pla-teau dwellers who got their name from a Sioux word: Shoo-*shoo*-nah, meaning "People who live in grass houses." With the coming of the horse to the Northwest in the middle of the previous century, the Shoshone ventured out onto the plains to become buffalo-hunting wanderers. In time they found life in towns where whiskey was readily available more to their liking. For the most part they got along fairly well with the white intruders, and elected to direct their hostility toward their hereditary enemies, the Crow and the Blackfoot.

DeLamar boasted but one hostelry, an outsized shack that advertised itself as the Bluebird House. One look at the place prompted Raider to suggest the name be changed to Buzzard's Roost. They shared a room on the top floor, returning to it after seeing to the horses for the night and enjoying their first hot meal in three days. Raider invested in a quart of rye, in his view a suitable substitute for the ill-fated bottle of Dr. Bloom's Cold Eradicator. Doc had little faith that rotgut would alleviate his affliction, but he refrained from comment. Raider proceeded to get roaring drunk, sick as a junkyard dog, and awoke in the morning feeling worse than ever.

They were having breakfast in a dingy and crowded diner across the street from the hotel when out the grimy window Doc spied Josh Kincaide. He put down his knife and fork and went out to greet him.

"I guessed you'd come over here," said the photographer. He fished in his pocket. "I knew you wouldn't be coming back to Silver City in a hurry. This wire came for you bright and early. Abel gave it to me."

Doc ripped open the envelope. "See that fellow sitting at the window table? That's my partner, Raider. He's still sick as a dog."

"Did you give him the Dr. Bloom's?"

Suddenly engrossed in the wire, Doc didn't answer. "Oh my Lord . . ."

"Trouble? They're not sending anybody to help you?"

"They're sending at least a dozen men, led by Operative Leroy Blodgett." Again Doc glanced at Raider. Despite his misery he was shoveling eggs and bacon into his mouth as rapidly as he could load his fork. "Maybe I'd better explain, Josh. My partner's an unusual man, a very good, capable, excellent operative, but he has very strong likes and dislikes."

"He doesn't like Leroy Blodgett."

"They thoroughly despise each other. To give you an idea how thoroughly, the last time the two of us were in Chicago, at the main office, Rade and I were sitting waiting for the chief to call us in when who should come parading through the door but Leroy. And I mean parading; he doesn't walk, doesn't march or even strut. He comes in like Queen Victoria in all her regal glory with an expression on his face like he's smelling rotten cheese. And when he spotted Raider he shriveled him with a look that would shatter glass. In ten seconds they were at it. Raider spoke his mind in greeting; I guess you could call it that. Leroy came snapping back. Then and there they would have started battering each other with their fists if I hadn't intervened; and if the chief hadn't come to the door and ordered us inside, graciously apologizing to Leroy for making him wait, which didn't help matters.

"The pity of it is—and the irony—the agency has a force of more than two hundred operatives. Of all the people to send us . . ."

"Does your Mr. Wagner have it in for you two?"

"It isn't William, it's Allan Pinkerton, and he doesn't have it in for us. He has this penchant for mixing unmixable personalities. He believes that under fire antagonists *learn* to get along. In his ideal scheme of things we're all brothers in the bond as fond of each other as Damon and Pythias. It's not the first time he's saddled us with Leroy, and it won'd be the last. Wait till Raider hears. Oh dear, oh my . . . Josh, I appreciate your bringing this over."

"Glad to." He looked toward Raider, who was still shoveling it in.

"Don't think me rude, but I'd rather you didn't stick around for the fireworks."

"What? Oh, of course not. I have to get back anyway. I've a business to run. I've an appointment in an hour for a group shot." He smirked. "Old friend of yours."

"Ira Pickett."

"And his gang."

"Do me a favor and print up an extra copy from the plate. It could come in handy for his wanted poster."

Raider took the news surprisingly well. Astonishingly. This was Doc's first reaction, and a wave of relief accompanied it, but looking into his partner's eyes he detected a strange gleam, prompting a most disturbing thought. Was Raider pleased that Leroy Blodgett was joining them? Did he look forward to getting him into the fray? Did he see it as a chance to do away with him? No. Raider wasn't like that. No question he despised the man, but he didn't want him dead. At least not by his hand. By some outlaw's? Possibly.

Probably. He thought about the war and the stories

about enlisted men who took advantage of the heat of battle to put a bullet in the back of an officer they hated. Raider would never do such a thing. It was beneath him. Still, that gleam in his eye . . .

Leroy Blodgett was a blueblood originally from Philadelphia; he traced his ancestors back to William Penn. He had been to the best private schools and had graduated with highest honors from the University of Pennsylvania. He was Raider's age—early thirties—outrageously handsome, blessed with a face that turned every female head around him. He was vain, he was a blowhard, he was overbearing, officious, insulting, and a snob, but he was good. He had courage, he was bright, he was resourceful —all in all a first-rate operative. Allan Pinkerton singled him out with pride as a prize acquisition, a man who could have been a rousing success in any career he chose, who had chosen the agency. The chief's inordinate fondness for him had its practical aspect: Blodgett attracted other well-educated, well-bred men to the ranks, so that no one could accuse the agency of harboring a flock of "fleabag gumshoes," third-rate, part-time policemen, full-time loafers.

Late that afternoon a second telegram arrived in Silver City to be forwarded by Abel Townsend to Mr. Weatherbee at the Bluebird House. Leroy Blodgett and the reinforcements would be arriving the next day. The Southern Pacific had reported that Aaron Cobble was dead. He had bled to death on the operating table while having his bullet removed.

"How could that be, Doc, that slug hit him in the shoulder!"

"Low and deep, Rade. Probably in the subclavian artery."

"The which?"

Doc traced it down his own shoulder. "It's as big as a hose. Still, it's surprising. Some doctor. Well, this gives us another count against Ira Pickett and his friends. I liked Aaron. He had grit."

"Salt o' the earth. Good-hearted, good-natured, he

could handle a gun, too. He couldn'ta been more'n nineteen or twenty, the bastards . . . When the hell are those boys gonna get here!"

"Don't get antsy. They'll show."

They waited the rest of the day and all the next day, but there was no sign of them, and no further telegrams. They had breakfast the third day then went back to their room. Raider was sitting at the foot of the bed, sneezing, voicing the empty claim that his cold was getting better, that he wasn't sneezing as often and "not near as snottily" when a sharp knock sounded at the door. They exchanged glances.

"Rade . . ."

"Yeah?"

"Behave yourself."

"Me? What about him? He's the one always starts it up."

"Whatever he says, let it go in one ear and out the other."

"Shit!"

"Please. You two are going to be stuck with each other till we wrap this up. Accept it. Don't bicker. If you bicker you'll argue, if you argue you'll fight, if you fight you may kill each other."

"Tell him, not me."

"Be big. Bigger than you've ever been before."

Another knock.

"Sticks and stones, Rade; ignore his insults and keep yours to yourself. I'm going to open the door. You be nice. Be gracious, friendly, civil; ask him how he is."

"Oh shut up!"

Doc sighed, went to the door, took a deep breath, let it out, and opened the door. There stood the chambermaid.

"You want your beds made up?"

Raider sniffed and chuckled.

"Not now, thank you, we'll be going out in a little bit."

Footsteps coming down the hall. It was a group led by an Adonis in a custom-tailored box-back Irish linen suit with a New York straw hat on his head, only partially concealing a host of golden curls reminiscent of General Custer's. The chambermaid looked at Leroy with mingled awe and adoration, caught herself, and fled.

"Leroy," said Doc mildly, extending his hand.

"Doc."

They shook hands. Leroy led his troop into the room, twelve in all, counting himself. He accorded Raider a curt nod, which Raider answered with the start of a sneer, checked aborning by a fierce glare from his partner. Introductions. Raider and Doc knew every man except for Loyal Dressler, who had just joined the agency and was on his first field assignment. He looked about seventeen and to Raider's disgust looked at Leroy the way a street urchin might look at Julius Caesar.

"Shades of Buckingham Palace," said Leroy looking around. "You do live well."

"This isn't Kansas City," said Doc. "It's the best this town has to offer. Shut the door, would you, Loyal? We'll fill you boys in on this mess."

Leroy took off his straw hat. The sunlight slanting through the window struck his hair, turning it to pure gold. He posed theatrically, elevating his chin and looking jaundicedly down his nose at Raider, who refused to look at him.

"Before you begin, Doc, we should get one thing straight." His eyes drifted to Raider. "I'm to be in charge."

"In a pig's asshole!" flared Raider.

"Rade . . ."

"I got a sudden nauseation in my stomach, Doc. I gotta go out and get me some fresh air. The stink in here is all of a sudden foul. You talk with Goldilocks, set him straight, don't take any o' his usual guff."

Doc scowled. "Stay where you are. Let's stop before you start, both of you."

"My dear fellow, I haven't said a blessed word to Mr. Hog Wallow."

"That's enough, Leroy. Cut it out, Rade, sit still. Leroy, one more word and I'll turn him loose on you, I mean it."

"I purely love you to do that, Doc ol' boy," he said, mimicking Raider's twang to perfection. "By jingo, by crackers, an' bet your boots, sure 'nough."

The others laughed. Raider reddened and started up from the bed. Face to face with Leroy he sneezed.

"You filthy swine!"

"It was a accident. Doc, you saw. I didn't even feel it comin' on, so help me. It was a accident, Goldilocks!"

"I ought to thrash you within an inch of your worthless life!"

"Let's go."

"Stop it!"

There was a long pause that fairly crackled, so tightly did the tension draw. It was broken when Leroy finished wiping his face with his monogrammed handkerchief. He smiled expansively. "You were saying, Doc?"

"This is our case, Leroy. I don't want to ruffle your feathers, believe me. Your help is enormously appreciated. Hopefully in the future we'll be able to reciprocate. I'm sure we will."

Leroy wasn't listening. He got out a paper, unfolded it, and held it for Doc to read. His eyes fell to the signature at the bottom.

"Orders direct from the chief," purred Leroy. "I'm to be in full charge. I didn't ask to be, word of honor. It's his idea. I couldn't very well disagree with him, could I? Besides, what's the difference who's in charge? We're all here for the same purpose, all on the same team."

Doc considered this a moment, then slowly nodded. "You're right."

"Bullshit!" burst Raider. "What the hell you tell him that for? What'sa matter with you, Weatherbee? Whatta ya suddenly got milk in your cods? Gimme that!" He snatched the chief's note from Leroy and ripped it to bits.

"Rade . . ."

"Don't say another word. You already said it all. You . . ." He looked about the gathering. "All o' you, do like you please. Let Goldilocks give the orders, you take 'em;

you too, Weatherbee. Count me the hell out!"

"Don't be ridiculous!" exclaimed Doc.

"I'm leavin'." He snatched up his saddlebags and started for the door, elbowing his way through the group. He jerked open the door and was gone, pounding down the hall. Doc threw up his hands.

Leroy leered. "To coin a phrase, Doc, good riddance to bad—"

"Don't say it, Leroy, not if you like your teeth in their present arrangement. You're in charge. I accept it. Just don't abuse it. Now listen closely. This is what we're up against."

CHAPTER FOUR

Raider sat sniffling, snuffling, wiping his nose with the back of his hand, seething, and nursing a tumbler of Valley Tan at a table in the rear of Grimshaw's Saloon and Gambling Emporium.

"A traitor, a damn Ben and Dick Arnold, that's what he is. Bad as both of 'em. Mr. Flasharity turned turncoat, a yellowbelly, yellow-back renegade for fair. I won't forget you for this, Weatherbee. I won't forgive you neither!"

"Got money in the bank, handsome?"

His eyes fixed on the contents of his glass, Raider looked up. "Whaa?"

"You're talking to yourself."

She was short, comfortably dumpy, twenty pounds overweight, but all in the right places. To one liberally powdered cheek clung a beauty mark the size of a penny. She was rather pretty through all the muck on her face, with auburn hair and sparkling green eyes. But he wasn't interested. Friendly conversation and an eventual romp in the hay were the furthest things from his mind. He had neither the energy nor the desire.

"Get lost, fatty!"

The green eyes exploded in instantaneous fury. "Who are you callin' fatty, pigsty? Look at you. You look like you been drug through a damn manure heap. You ever take a bath in your life? Ever shave? Pig! *Pig!*"

"How'd you like to go flyin' over the bar face first, ass after, you bigmouth tub o' lard!"

A burly waiter, his apron scandalously filthy, his fists formed, a scowl tightening his bulldog face, came bustling up. "What's goin' on here?"

"This walkin' pigsty insulted me!" exclaimed the lady.

"I did like hell. You lie in your fat rotten teeth! She come bargin' up, nobody asked her, blowin' off at the face. Get outta here, you disgustin' cow, and take your mutt-face friend with ya!"

The waiter bristled, his eyes firing. "You're the one's gettin' outta here, cannon mouth. On your feet and beat it, b'fore I bust you up."

"Tell him, Walter. Give it to him! Beat him bowlegged!"

"Shut up, Althea Mae."

"Yeah, shut up, Althea Mae. Fatass!" Raider lurched to his feet to the happy discovery that he towered over the waiter. Walter lifted his eyes slowly, cringing slightly but perceptibly. "I'm leavin'. I'm choosy who I give my business to. This rathole's the bottom o' the trash barrel. Ya oughta be 'shamed and mortified you work here, Walter. Whyn'cha hang this ball o' lard out back and let the grackles pick at it; gettin' her outta sight won't hurt your business none, you betcha."

He left, all eyes following him out and Althea Mae's insults slamming his eardrums, sparking laughter, encouragement, and scattered applause. He stood outside, sniffling and slowly simmering down. To hell with turncoat Weatherbee, with Goldilocks Blodgett and the Pinkertons. To hell with A.P.

"I'll show ya all. Most 'specially you, Weatherbee. I'll clean this mess up one-handed. Wind it up all by myself alone!"

He walked around the side of the saloon and sat down on the ground, his back against the wall. By now Abington would surely have warned Pickett that Pinkertons were after him; at that, even if he hadn't gotten around to telling him, Mr. Stink'd have to expect they would be. You don't hold up a Southern Pacific train, kill innocents, and get away without the agency climbing on your tail. Pickett was no greenhorn, he knew the ropes and the rules, and likely wrote half of them. And he'd seen him and Doc inside the car just before he cold-cocked them. He'd recognize him in two shakes.

"What I need is a disguise. Old A.P. 'd purely love that; grouchy old penny-pincher's big on disguises. That's what I'll do, disguise myself, go back to Silver City, find Pickett, collar him, and lock him up back here, anyplace but there. With him outta the game, Doc and Goldilocks can mop up the rest like sittin' in a easy chair. He's the big cheese, and he's mine. You're finished, Mr. Stink, y'hear?"

What would he disguise himself as? An Indian walked by, his hair in braids, head down, moccasined feet shuffling, his blanket wrapped tightly about him. He looked ancient but was probably no older than Allan Pinkerton, Raider decided. He got to his feet, dusted off his rear, and leaned out and followed him with his eyes. Half a block up the street he encountered two more Indians. They began jabbering.

"That's it, Raider. A Indian."

An ideal disguise. Perfect. Indians were all over town, but they might just as well be wooden and holding a fistful of coronas for all the attention people gave them. They were there, but nobody noticed.

Appraising himself in a store window, Raider decided the first thing he'd have to get rid of was his mustache. He could do without a braid wig; his hair was jet black and fell almost to his shoulders. He could bunch it either side and bind it with strips of rawhide the way old Chief Washakie did. He could pick up a soft buckskin shirt with fringed sleeves and fringed trousers, along with a blanket from any one of half a dozen squat peddlers on the sidewalk. They were all over town, as they were in Silver City, peddling souvenirs, jewelry, blankets, and beadwork, some even clay cook pots. Moccasins would be easy to acquire too, and he'd need a lanyard ornamented with a shell or metal disk, or maybe a cougar claw necklace for around his neck.

The big thing was his face, his skin; luckily his cheekbones were high and his eyes Indian brown. He was much too tall for a Shoshone, but if anybody's suspicions were aroused on that score they could take him for a Cheyenne. Some Crows grew above six foot, too. Another good thing about posing as an Indian was that he could stand two feet away from white men talking and hear everything they said and they'd never give him a second look, the way they would another white man.

All in all his skin appeared to be his only problem, his face, neck, and hands the only exposed parts. He went hunting for a drugstore, found Gourad's Apothecary, and bought a large tube of Pozzoni's Stage Makeup Cream— No. 17 Bronze, Plains Indian, and some Blue Seal Vaseline and cotton balls. He also bought a bottle of Dr. Bloom's Cold Eradicator.

He only knew half a dozen Shoshone words; he'd rely on sign language in a pinch. Indians grunted a lot, too, especially the older ones. Yes, he could sign his way through a conversation if conversation was unavoidable.

He would also need a pony blanket for his horse and twenty feet of rope to fashion a war bridle to replace his hackamore and reins. Tying a lark's-head knot around his horse's lower jaw was simple; it formed the bit, and the rope ends served as reins. As far as his horse went, he saw only one problem, which with any luck would never betray him—the fact that she was shod, a luxury of the trail no Indian ever bothered with.

He could leave his saddlebags and sleeping bag with the manager of the livery stable where his horse was boarded. He could pack his .45 under his shirt inside his belt.

"Yes, sir, this is gonna' be a A-one disguise. Weatherbee passin' me on the street won't recognize me. And Pickett won't for sure!"

Doc rode abreast of Leroy Blodgett, leading the other operatives out to the Patchett ranch. Doc mentally crossed his fingers, praying that Pickett and his gang would still be squatting there, and when the house came into view and the corral was filled with horses as before, his heart glowed in relief.

"There it is."

Blodgett pulled up, signaling the others to a halt. They crowded around as he surveyed the area. The landscape was virtually barren of cover, the area to the north, reaching to Silver City beyond, fanning out as flat as a stove lid, offering scattered clumps of sagebrush and other, even leaner vegetation that could barely hide a single attacker. The men began checking their rifles and pistols.

"What do you think, Doc?"

"I don't know. If we surround them and open up we'll just be inviting a Mexican standoff. We won't draw them out, and they won't draw us any closer. There'll be a lot of noise, a lot of wasted ammunition, and four hours from now when night falls we'll both have to quit."

"Not necessarily. If we got hold of a wagonload of hay, pushed it up to the back door there, and set fire to it . . ."

"That'd be pretty risky, Leroy. There's not even a slight grade; whoever does the pushing will be sitting ducks for their men posted at the back windows."

"Any ideas?"

"One, for starters. Wait till dark, sneak up on the corral, and chase out their horses."

"I don't see as they would help us any. It's thirty or

forty feet from the back door of the corral gate. Two men could easily cover it with rifles. They'd have to run a gauntlet of firing just to reach the gate, then unfasten and open it. Even at this distance a halfway decent shot would drop anyone who tried it in their tracks. They'd barely get out the door. Bother the horses. I say we take the bull by the horns and get at it—surround them and start the show."

"You're the boss."

Blodgett eyed him and licked his lips. Doc read his expression as that of one experiencing sudden second thoughts. He'd asked him for his opinion; he'd given it only to have it rejected, in effect putting Blodgett on his own. If they attacked successfully and routed the outlaws, he'd end up with a nice bright and shiny feather for his cap; if, as he had pointed out, they started shooting and wound up in a standoff, egg on his face would replace the feather. In the eyes of the others, certainly, even if it didn't get back to Chicago. The devil in Doc urged him to push, nudge Leroy onto the spot as, if nothing else, a small favor to Raider. Leroy wanted to be leader, the chief had designated him leader, let him lead.

Do something.

"What'll it be?" Doc asked. He eyed Blodgett questioningly, striving for innocence in his expression, at the same time determined to make him feel uncomfortable. Everyone was staring expectantly at Leroy. He licked his lips again, ran one gloved hand through his golden locks, and fidgeted. Doc was hard put to suppress a smile; he could not keep from laughing inwardly. And thinking that if Raider were there he'd come up with something clever and eminently workable. He almost never failed to. Such situations were his dish of tea. Even Allan Pinkerton himself deferred to his judgment, experience, and expertise on such occasions. But Raider was elsewhere. Where he'd gotten to, what he was up to, if anything, begged the wildest of wild guesses.

"I'll bet he's up to something," murmured Doc.

Blodgett frowned. "What?"

"Nothing. Well, shall we start or take the time to explore further possible strategies? To be honest, I don't see a one. Do you?"

Blodgett cleared his throat and tried a glare. Let's go. We'll surround them. I'll fire the first shot. That'll be the signal to open up. Throw everything we've got in the first volley."

"We may get lucky and hit somebody," said Doc dryly.

Blodgett glared in earnest.

CHAPTER FIVE

Raider stood in front of Hurtlemeyer's Cash Store next door to Sheriff Nat Abington's office. He had not moved in more than an hour, and in that time had overheard snatches of no fewer than six conversations alluding to outlaw activities interspersed with ordinary conversation and gossip from passersby. His Shoshone Indian garb and disguise had long since passed the acid test of close-up observation. He had taken special pains with his makeup, and he now turned around to glance in the window at it, reacting proudly. The telegrapher seated at his key in his shirtsleeves and green visor smiled, winked, and mimed hooting, rapping his rounded mouth with his fingers.

"You go to hell," muttered Raider. "I bet you make fun o' all us Indians."

Sheriff Abington came out of his office accompanied by an older man on crutches.

"They got away with nearly six thousand," said the man. "You know the bank in DeLamar."

"It's a cracker box," responded Abington, leering. "A

handful o' little kids could turn it over. Anybody keeps his money there oughta have his head examined."

"Ain't it the truth. Like I say, Ira disguised him and the boys like Injuns." Raider perked up his ears. "If he ain't a card. Anythin' for a laugh. Weren't but five of 'em. They got clean away. Last I seen they was headin' north."

"Hope he's got sense 'nough not to double back and wind up out to Patchett's. That'd be the first place anybody chasin' him'd look."

"If they knowed it was him done it. Dressed up like a Injun, how could they?"

"How'd you hear 'bout it, Arthur?"

"I was there. I saw it. That bowlegged little varmint could dress up and make himself up like U.S. Grant's wife, Julia. A blind man could see through it if you know him. The way he walks hunched over, them steer-rib legs, the way he cants his head to one side. Hell, I said hello when he rode by. 'Hello, Ira.' I did."

Abington laughed heartily. Raider thought a moment, made up his mind, and, still holding his arms folded under his blanket in the accepted pose of the race, turned and padded down the alley to his waiting horse. If Ira Pickett wouldn't come to him, he'd go to Ira Pickett.

Leroy Blodgett and his men and Doc lay flat on their bellies a good two hundred yards from the target. It struck Doc that a buzzard's-eye view of them would be that of a gigantic clock with thirteen slender black indicators in place of numbers. But for all the considerable risk it entailed, offering next to no cover, Blodgett's frontal attack was proving somewhat effective. Mostly because the defending outlaws were rashly exposing themselves now and again in order to get a better shot at the Pinkertons. Six yells totaled six casualties, perhaps half that number killed, the others wounded. From the amount of gunfire being poured back at them, Doc deduced that the outlaws' ranks had been thinned since his and Raider's previous visit to the area. He counted only fifteen horses in the corral, when before there had been close to twice that number.

The battle had passed the twenty-minute mark. Two operatives had been hit, one badly, taking a slug straight into his chest when he carelessly raised upward to see if he'd hit his target. He had failed to, and was shot in retaliation. He was dying. He was three men over on Doc's left. Blodgett was positioned next over, and the first man on his other side was the new recruit, young and untried Loyal Dressler. His complexion was normally pale; at the moment it was ashen. Small wonder: he was the second casualty, one slug knocking his derby from his head, a second grazing his hairline. All the men on either side Doc could see had taken the precaution of hilling up whatever loose dirt they could find in front of them. It wasn't much protection, but if they were careful and kept their heads down, as the mortally wounded man had not, the outlaws would see only their rifles and their hands.

It was at times like these, Doc reflected morosely, that one would give one's eyeteeth for a ravine, at least a rain ditch, a boulder, a dead horse, anything to curl up behind and feel some small sense of security. The only thing approaching security was not each man's individual hillocks nor his flattening, but the considerable distance separating the combatants. If the Pinkertons moved closer, to say a hundred yards, as Blodgett had suggested at the start, the men inside would wipe them out in sixty seconds.

The shadows lengthened as the sun dipped lower, becoming redder and redder and gradually assuming the color of fresh blood. The badly wounded man quietly died. Loyal Dressler was hit a second time, through no fault of his making that Doc could see, a slug plowing into the point of his right shoulder, a very lucky shot. He screamed and wrenched upward.

"Oh my God . . ." murmured Doc.

A fatal mistake. A follow-up shot drove into his chest and out his back, tearing and lifting the material of his jacket.

"Two down," muttered Doc and flattened further, mentally imbedding himself in the hard dry ground to a safe depth of twelve inches. His hat lay four feet from him to his right. One of them got a bead on it and drilled it cleanly. Pressing his right ear to the ground, Doc pivoted his head on it for a look at the sun. It was almost touching the horizon. Another twenty minutes and it would slip below it. Eventually night would descend and the windows in view would fill with lamplight. They should have waited till dark to begin the attack; they wouldn't have lost the two, the boy in his baptism of fire. That was one the chief would inquire about when Blodgett's report went into the case journal. Allan Pinkerton dreaded and hated losing a man; losing a recruit, one on whose I.D. card the ink was barely dry, desolated him. He was the one who contacted the wives and mothers and other relatives. He wrote the letter, expressing his personal regrets, suffering through every stroke of the pen.

"This is getting us nowhere," groused Blodgett.

Doc was tempted to say "I told you so," but held his peace. The two deaths had shaken the man. It was as if going in he hadn't expected they would suffer any casualties. Neither wise nor sensible, considering the situation; and giving the devil his due, Leroy Blodgett was wise and sensible. Only this time too eager, too bold.

"What do you say we hold our fire, save our ammunition until dark," suggested Doc. Blodgett grunted in response. "Is that yes or no?"

"And when it does get dark?"

He was looking past Doc at the Dressler boy lying crumpled on his side, his left leg drawn up, raising his hip, his pale blue eyes staring, his mouth open, blood glistening, trickling down into the sand.

Doc, his cheek pressed against the ground, shifted his eyes to study the sky. "I'm afraid there'll be stars and the moon. It won't be as bright as day, but bright enough. They'll be expecting us to move up, of course."

"Of course."

"What if two or three of us started forward from one side, say the west, crouching, running, dropping, crouching, running, dropping, converging, throwing heavy fire at them. It might draw most of them to the front. The rest of you could approach the corral in a straight line to the rear. The horses would block sight of you. You could fan out on either side of the corral, sticking close to it, and blast away. Possibly even rush the back door. And if it drew men from the front, hopefully we could make it to the front door."

"It sounds terribly risky."

"It can't be any riskier than this," bawled the man on Blodgett's other side, the boy lying dead between them. "Makes sense to me, only count me out for the three coming up front. That's suicide."

"I'll have a go at it," said Doc grimly.

A man sprawled out three over to his right carelessly lifted his arm to volunteer. Two quick shots forced it back down, narrowly missing it.

"We'll need one more," said Doc.

He perceived that he would have to wait until dark for his next volunteer if indeed he'd get one; the others in the buzzard's clock were well out of earshot.

Raider made it to within sight of DeLamar in short order. He skirted the little town, cutting north. He pushed the mare hard; four or five miles north of town she began fighting for breath. They had begun climbing into the Owyhee Mountains. Tiny Reynolds beckoned. The horse was winded. She stumbled. Raider pulled up so sharply he nearly went flying head over heels. He got down and patted her muzzle. She was heavily lathered.

"Did I overdo you, little girl? I'm sorry. Emergency. I wouldn't do it if I didn't have to. Catch your breath, there's a good girl."

He looked about for water, but there was none. He walked her forward to keep her from cramping. She was tossing her head as if in appreciation of his stopping. Her nostrils flared as she sucked her lungs full of the hot dry air.

"Maybe they stopped in Reynolds. I wouldn't. Not when you can get up into the hills and find a hundred places to hole up."

Every one as easy to defend as a stone fort. He heard hoofbeats. A host of riders was approaching, coming from the direction of Reynolds.

"It's him!"

He dug under his shirt for his gun. He got it out, but before he could lift it and aim, two shots came blasting at him, bracketing him where he stood.

"Drop it!"

He dropped it. They came barreling up, quickly surrounding him.

"He's one of 'em, Calvin," said the runt with skin as dark as Raider's No. 17 Bronze, Plains Indian makeup.

The leader roughly resembled Abington, only he was older and, Raider assumed, no protector of Indians. Everyone was glaring pitchforks at him.

"Pipe the getup," the runt went on. "Did you ever see anythin' more foolisher-lookin'? You look 'bout as much like a Injun as Lola Montez, Chrissakes."

Others echoed this assessment.

"String him up!"

"Shoot him! 'Sfaster. Let's get outta here."

"Wait a minute," flared Raider.

"Where's the money?" Calvin glared. "You got no saddlebags, where'd you stash it?"

"I got no money, I didn't rob any dumb bank, I can prove it!"

"You're one of 'em, got to be."

"String him up!"

A noose had been readied and was brought forward. Calvin snatched it from the man and looked about for a tall tree.

Raider swallowed. "You hay pitchers are makin' the

biggest mistake 'o your lives!" he boomed.

"String him up!"

"Wait, wait," exclaimed another man. He pushed alongside Calvin. "He's one, he must know where the others are."

"That's so," said Calvin.

"That's bullshit," said Raider. "I'm not one, I'm after 'em same as you."

"*That's* bullshit!" snapped the runt and sneered at Raider. "Let's get the sumabitch to dancin'."

"It's the damn truth, you sawed-off jackass. Ira Pickett's the leader. He's the one I'm after. I'm a Pinkerton."

"You're a liar!"

"String him up!"

Raider scowled fiercely. "Little runt, how come you talk so much and don't say a damn thing worth listenin' to? How come you boys let him? How come you didn't leave him home to hold the knittin' yarn for his ma?" His eyes drifted from one face to the next. "I'll prove I'm tellin' the truth. Here's my I.D."

"String him up!"

Calvin took it from him. "Operative Raider," he read. "Number twenty-four. That's what it says, boys."

"He stole it, Calvin," said the runt. "What are we wastin' time jawin' for? Gimme that noose!"

"Why would I steal a Pinkerton I.D., for Chrissakes?"

"To pass yourself off as one," said Calvin. "What else?"

"String him up!"

"I been passin' myself off as one for eleven years. Bigmouth's got one thing right, we're wastin' time. Pickett and his pals are up into the Owyhees by now, either barricaded in or hid out where the whole Department o' the Missouri Army could never find 'em."

"We're still goin' after 'em," said Calvin resolutely. He tossed back the I.D. "He's got no money, he says he's a Pink, I believe him. Not 'cause he says he is, not 'cause the money's not on him, but on account he's made up too good, greasepaint and all. They was only buckskins and feathers when they hit the bank. They didn't go through Reynolds. Let's cut over to Murphy and see if we can pick up on 'em. We're gonna have to scour the hills from the border down to Braineau. You wanta come and lend a hand, Chief?"

"I'm comin'! I'm comin'!"

CHAPTER SIX

The idea in the planning was a daring one, reflected Doc sourly, but in execution it was foolhardy. Had there been halfway decent cloud cover it might work, but the moon was nearly full and surrounded by legions of twinkling stars, lighting up the landscape so brightly one could easily read a newspaper. One could easily spot anybody sneaking up on them.

He had always considered himself middling brave. Not a coward, no daredevil. Under stress he sweat adequately; his heart usually pounded louder than normal, but not so powerfully his breastbone was in danger of shattering. His biggest problem was the light and the edge it gave the outlaws inside. And his unignorable common sense. It fairly shouted "Don't try it, don't be an idiot, you haven't a chance in hell of making it to the door. You won't get ten yards before they cut you down." Nevertheless, he had to go through with it; one doesn't back out of one's own suggestion; he might as well hang a large red sign saying "Coward " around his neck. One doesn't back out when the two others are willing to go through with it.

"Fools."

He took the center lane. They took up their positions about two hundred yards from the front door, thirty yards between them. Doc hesitated a long moment to give Blodgett and the others out back plenty of time to begin their approach to the corral. He counted to thirty, then raised his arm and brought it back down sharply. They started forward, crouching low. The outlaws' view was unobstructed; what sagebrush survived in the hard dry ground rose barely a foot in height. All but useless as cover even lying prone.

Doc stiffened. Any second now they would open up, a furious barrage, ten seconds with ten rifles blasting, cutting them down like wheat.

They had covered fifty yards when the night silence shattered; the boys at the back had opened up. A filmy cloud of gunsmoke slowly rose above the house. The occupants were returning fire. To Doc's amazement and indescribable relief not a single shot came their way. Blodgett's timing was perfect. Seemingly every man inside had run to the rear to defend against an attempt to rush the back door. The din was deafening. Doc and the other two were straight up now, running forward, converging on the front door. Their rifles were cocked and ready, but not one of them fired. Up to the door they rushed. It was locked.

"Bolted, too, I bet," rasped the man on his left.

Doc had pressed his shoulder against it; he eased back. "The window there."

The firing out back continued heavy. Doc smashed the window with his rifle butt. They climbed inside and began raking the parlor. Not a living soul remained in the house. They could see through to the kitchen. The back door gaped wide. They rushed toward it, banging shoulders in their haste. By the time they reached it the firing outside had subsided; the corral gate was wide, the outlaws mounted up and thundering away, leaving their dead and wounded and Pinkerton casualties strewn about the yard. Three operatives were up on their knees and firing after the fleeing men. Leroy Blodgett came staggering toward Doc. Blood oozed through his jacket from a shoulder wound. He had lost his hat, his golden curls were in disarray, his eyes gaped. He appeared to be in shock but was coherent.

"It was a solid wall of lead. I've never seen anything like it. We were moving down the sides of the pen. The boys up front opened fire. They threw it back at us. It was like grapeshot."

Men lying on the ground around them groaned. Two raised upward. A third tried to and fell back down. A hasty check of casualties verified that two more operatives had been killed and one badly wounded, gut-shot, and not likely to survive into the next hour only three minutes away. The wounded were able to walk and mount their horses, although one man hit in the thigh was bleeding badly. A tourniquet was quickly applied, stanching the flow, and his horse was brought up with the others. He was lifted into the saddle.

Six outlaws had been killed in the breakout. Three others lay dead in the kitchen. Two wounded never made it to their horses. One, suffering only a flesh wound in the hand, was brought forward to be questioned.

"Where are they heading?" asked Blodgett.

"Go to hell."

Blodgett slapped him smartly with his glove. "Talk!"

"Silver City, where else? They'll be safe there." He leered. "You can't touch 'em. Nobody can, not even the Army."

"Where's Pickett?" Doc asked.

"Gone."

Again Blodgett slapped him. He staggered back, his wounded hand going to his cheek. "What the hell . . ." He glanced at Doc appealingly, as if hoping he would intercede in his behalf. "Him and some o' the boys went off this afternoon."

Doc glared. "Where? For what?"

"To rob the bank in DeLamar."

"They'll be coming back here," Doc said to Blodgett.

"No they won't," said the outlaw. "They're gone for good. Don't ask me where, they wouldn't say. Ira don't tell us nothin'. Him and his two boys and Willis McColl and Asa Hudlin, they stick together like Diamond glue. Rest of us only been with 'em a couple months. The five o' them been together years." He was staring fixedly at Doc. "I'm tellin' you the bald truth. I know they went to rob the DeLamar bank, but after that God only knows where they're headin' to."

Blodgett surveyed the battlefield. "A minor massacre. As pointless, as unfruitful as it was bloody. Let's start cleaning up. We'll bury the dead, send our wounded on ahead to Silver City, and take this one and the other with us when we leave."

"Not to Silver City," said Doc. "We turn them over to Sheriff Abington and he'll let them out the minute our backs are turned."

Blodgett sniffed. "We can lock him up with them."

"Easier said than done, I'm afraid. It's a bad situation, but not our concern, not at the moment."

It was agreed to remove the two wounded prisoners to DeLamar, then regroup and go after Pickett and his core gang. Catching them would also be easier said than done, mused Doc. They had six hours' head start. In unfamiliar mountainous territory at night.

Calvin Henshaw's determination turned out more talk than effort. With Raider tagging along, riding alongside the runt and continuing to exchange unpleasantries with him, the posse set out for Murphy. When they got there they found no trace of Pickett and his tribe; no one in town had seen either white men masquerading as Indians or unfamiliar white men, either group in a hurry. Henshaw took one last long look at the surrounding mountain peaks and holstered the gun of his resolve.

"It's useless, boys. Worse than lookin' for a needle in a haystack."

Raider snapped. "You're givin' up so soon?"

"What's the use?" asked the runt. Others nodded.

"That bowlegged little misfit robs your bank and you let him get away with it?"

Calvin was beginning to look sheepish. He shrugged. "What can we do? It's gettin' dark, gettin' late, I'm gettin' hungry."

"Oh for Chrissakes!" Raider glared his way from one face to the next. "Okay, quit if you want to, but not me. He's around here, I can almost smell his stink. He'll stick around, too. He pays that sheriff in Silver City to protect him; he won't run out from under his wing. Maybe he didn't ride through Reynolds or here or any other town, but they headed north. They got to be up in these mountains someplace. Or run back to Silver City. There's just the one road east o' here cuts back south to there. They coulda run straight for that road, never mind the mountains. Now I think about it, that's what I'd do."

"He's got it all figgered out," said the runt. He began to cackle.

"That's it," said Raider. "Laugh hard enough and you might laugh the ugly off your face, you sawed-off asshole! Laugh till your scrawny ribs ache, it still makes sense. I'm goin' on."

"I wish you luck," said Calvin. "You do have a point about Pickett not strayin' too far from Silver City. Could be he's back already. Which is the best reason why we should call it off. If he's back under Abington's protection we can't touch him. It's an old story round here. We been livin' with it for six years."

"That's your problem, not mine. I'll get Pickett, his friends, and that bent tin star. I'll see the whole mangy lot behind bars, and when they're hauled up in front o' the judge and all their dirty laundry is hung up for everybody to see, you boys make sure you come around. I'll see you get front row seats." He spat. "Beat it, go home to your beans and your old ladies. Get down in your boots and hide. You make me sick!"

He wheeled about and rode off. Silver City it was, he

decided. Sooner or later and likely sooner Mr. Stink would come back. One good thing seemed to have happened—in all the excitement his cold seemed to be on the wane. Whether it was the Dr. Bloom's or the passage of time he couldn't say, but he'd stopped sneezing and his nose was no longer stuffed up.

Doc and Leroy Blodgett brought their two prisoners to DeLamar for temporary lodging. The marshall made no effort to mask his reluctance to take them. It was plain to Doc that he preferred not to meddle in something that could invite the wrath of the sheriff. DeLamar was an honest town, and Marshal Watts was capable and uncorrupted, but the robbers roost that was Silver City was too close and Nat Abington too powerful not to pose a threat. Watts only accepted the prisoners on the promise that they would be returned to Nevada and Elko, where they would stand trial within forty-eight hours or less.

The Pinkerton who had been shot in the stomach had died on the ride to DeLamar. The four other, less seriously wounded men were taken to a local doctor. The other bodies, including Loyal Dressler's, were removed to the undertaker's. The exhausted survivors dragged themselves off to bed. Doc and Leroy stood on the veranda of the Bluebird House smoking and talking. The events of the evening had shattered Blodgett; young Dressler's death in his very first action devastated him. He did not elaborate on why he was taking the tragedy so hard. To Doc he didn't have to. Allan Pinkerton had assigned Dressler to the case, putting him under Blodgett's wing in the confidence that he would be training on the job with one of the best. Including Raider and Weatherbee among his mentors would also have been in the chief's thinking. In his eleven years with the agency Doc could not recall a similar instance when a recruit was killed his first time under fire. It had probably happened, but he personally knew of no such case.

Blodgett puffed on his stogie and stared through the

smoke at the moon that had joined the enemy against them.

"It never felt right from the beginning, did it?" Blodgett said.

Doc shook his head in agreement.

"We never should have circled them the way we did, even at that distance. There was just no bloody cover, none!"

He was getting angry. At himself. He felt the full weight of responsibility, and he should, mused Doc. But to his credit Blodgett made no effort to shift some of it to his or other shoulders. The chief would want all the particulars; Blodgett would have to provide them. Others who had taken part would be called in and questioned. Anytime operatives were killed or gravely wounded there was an official investigation. It was a situation that begged second-guessing; the chief would second-guess it to death. As always his rationale would be that "we learn from our mistakes; doing so helps prevent future casualties." It sounded plausible, even logical, but it was neither simply because no two confrontations were alike, and the strategy and conduct best for one, and tailored for it, no more fit another than one man's suit of clothes fit another without a tuck here and an alteration there.

"What could we have done that would have been better or safer, Doc?"

He was already preparing for his visit to Allan Pinkerton's carpet. He would be called upon to explain his reasons for his actions, just that, not called in to be castigated. The chief didn't do that. From his point of view it made no sense. All it would do was lower morale and give those in charge second thoughts about their plans of action. Indecision would come to be the norm. Nevertheless, like every other man placed in charge of an operation, Blodgett would have to submit to questioning. It promised to be no worse than what he was undergoing at the moment: questions asked by him of him.

"I don't know, Leroy," responded Doc. "Given a little more time to think the thing out we might have come up with a different approach. I say 'might have,' but I don't necessarily think we would have. As you say, the lack of cover made it terrifically hard. They had all they needed, and we had none."

He was trying to reassure him and ease his mind without being obvious about it, sticking to the facts as both knew them, trying to ease the pain the man was feeling and help dismiss the second thoughts that were arriving like a swarm of bees to assail and torment him.

"I hope you're not just saying that."

"Not at all. Leroy, we can't talk it to death, we'll just start repeating ourselves. Look at it this way, there's not a man who was out there who doesn't know in his heart that we did all that could be done under extremely trying circumstances. I don't see how we could have done anything differently; less bloodily, if you will. And think about this, we could have had it a whole lot worse."

"That's true." This last seemed to give him a small lift.

"Let's call it a night," said Doc.

Blodgett tossed his stogie into the street and nodded. They turned and started in. "I wonder what happened to Raider?" Blodgett said. "I'm sure he's off fishing by himself."

Doc nodded, wondering as he did so what indeed Raider was up to.

As the hours dragged on, daylight waned and darkness came down from the mountain. The lights were being turned on in Silver City. Raider was feeling more and more foolish in his makeup and regalia. For all the pains he had taken he had not fooled Calvin or any of his men close up.

True to his words to them, he had returned to Silver City, but neither Pickett nor any of his men were about. Raider searched the town, wandering into every saloon, dance hall, and gambling casino, but there was no sign of them. He did bump into Sheriff Abington—twice. It pleased him when Abington failed to recognize him. Seeing Abington the first time summoned up thoughts of his counterpart in DeLamar. Marshall Watts and his deputies had left the chase to Calvin and his vigilantes; Watts and his men had not set foot out of their office. Curiously, the people of DeLamar appeared to understand and accept his reluctance to chase. If he had and had captured Pickett he'd have to bring him back and lock him up—and expect Abington to come calling shortly. Eventually the prisoners would have to be turned over to his custody, since Silver City was the county seat and he was the ranking peace officer in the county. So to Watts what was the point in capturing them?

It was bad enough that Abington controlled Silver City but his influence reached into the surrounding towns and hamlets too.

"It's downright disgustin'. Somebody oughta put a flea in the governor's ear."

Disgusting it was, and as such lent even more importance to *his* capturing Pickett and his men. He'd herd them down to Elko County in Nevada for trial. The area newspapers would have a field day. It couldn't help but bring Abington's corruption out into the open. When he got wind of it, Governor Bennett would be as outraged as he was embarrassed.

"He'll stomp Abington out like a cockroach."

It was becoming increasingly clear that Pickett, whatever his reason might be, was in no hurry to get back to Silver City. Had he gone directly to the Patchett ranch? He'd be in for a surprise if he did. By now Blodgett, Doc, and the others must have hit it. Raider resolved to ride out for a look.

He found the place in darkness, the corral empty, one gate hinge broken, the back door wide open. Nobody was about. Blodgett and Doc seemed to have succeeded in routing the outlaws who had remained behind when Pickett and the others left to rob the bank. Solely out of a sense of orderliness Raider closed the back door and shut the corral gate. He then remounted and trotted out. He had not put a mile between himself and the house when he heard hoofbeats up ahead. Dropping his blanket on his horse's rump, he got out his .45 and held it in readiness by his right leg.

Whoever was coming appeared to be headed for the house. He pulled well off the road. Anyone riding by looking in his direction would have spotted him, but the five who galloped past, like himself in Indian getup, were too busy talking to look. He let them get well by, then followed.

He pulled up and watched from a distance as they dismounted and led their horses into the corral, laughing and talking loudly until one discovered the broken hinge. That seemed to draw more attention than the corral's being empty. Perhaps, he thought, they assumed everyone had gone into town.

He waited till they were milling around the gate and beginning to close it, then slapped his horse into a sudden full gallop and sped up to them so fast they began running in all directions for fear of being trampled. He got off a warning shot and ordered them to freeze. Four did so without hesitation; one refused to. Pickett. He was halfway between the corral and the back door. Instead of stopping with the others, he spun about and raced headlong back to the corral. So surprised was Raider, by the time he got a shot off Pickett was climbing through the bars in among the horses. One of the others took advantage of the distraction and pulled his gun. Raider spotted him, but not before he was able to get off a wild shot, grazing Raider's horse's neck, frightening her so she went crazy, rising on her hind legs, nearly tossing him, whirling about and racing away.

Bound by the war bridle, he nearly pulled her lower jaw off before he could settle her down—but not until he was a good hundred yards from the corral. The outlaws, standing watching, lost no time in seizing the advantage. Four ran for the cover of the house, while the fifth mounted and came after Raider.

"I'm gonna git you, Injun!" he bawled shrilly.

Pickett. Raider heeled the mare and took off. Let him follow, he thought. He'd lead him around Silver City, back the way they'd come, up into the Owyhees. Up a mountain trail he could easily double back on without being seen and come up on him from behind.

Still, Mr. Stink was a slick one. He'd proven that. This could turn out to be his last chance to lay hands on him. He knew Pinkertons were following him up from Thunder Mountain, knew too that if they caught him he'd face not just holdup charges but murder. Cornered he wouldn't hesitate to shoot. He had nothing to lose and the rest of his misbegotten life to gain.

Raider led him a hectic chase past the lights of Silver City, glowing dully to their left, into the foothills and up into the mountains. Higher and higher both horses legged it. with no sign of a side trail. Pickett had yet to get off a shot. Raider reloaded as he rode, fumbling with his shells, losing three overboard, cursing the next two into their chambers.

The trail zigzagged upward at one corner then another, presenting sheer drops of three to four hundred feet. Pickett pushed his horse. Raider could hear him rein-strapping it, but the outlaw could not close the gap separating them. In frustration, wearied of bawling empty threats, he began shooting. So rugged was the terrain, so difficult to get and hold a bead on a moving target, only a lucky shot would find its mark; but Raider was unwilling to settle for even the most favorable odds.

He had to get out of range or out of sight. He was sure of one thing: all the threats Pickett had thrown at him so far confirmed that he had no idea who he was chasing.

Raider came to fork, cut left, changed his mind, and pulled the horse right. The abrupt change in direction caused her to stumble and nearly fall. He could have been thrown, but he alertly shifted his weight, keeping himself in the saddle. He rounded a boulder, escaping sight of his pursuer, threw himself down, and slapped the mare's rump, sending her scooting farther up the way. He scrambled up onto the boulder, flattening and bringing his gun around. He could hear the rattle of gravel below. He spotted Pickett's El Tavor hat bobbing. He let fly and blew it off, the chin cord catching him in the throat. He gagged, bellowed, and began blasting wildly. Raider flattened. Slugs sang over him, ticking his boulder, striking the wall at his back and bouncing harmlessly off it. He returned fire. By now Pickett had reached the fork. Instead of following Raider to the right, he pushed his mount left. In a second he was out of sight behind an outcropping. Raider twisted a quarter turn to his right and waited expectantly for him to emerge into view. He could hear him but could not see a hair. He could also hear the Snake River rushing through the rocks five hundred feet down at the base of the range on the far side.

He waited, gun cocked, ready, muzzle following the path he guessed the outlaw was taking. He had yet to see any sign of him, nor could he hear him anymore. He strained his ears. Only the breeze and the churning water below sent him their sounds.

"Son of a bitch!"

He slid down the boulder feet first and ran for his horse. He rode on up the trail. Moments later he emerged from between two upright slabs and glanced down. The Snake white-watered its way toward the Oregon border. The trail down was steep—a nearly vertical drop. He took a deep breath, tightened his legs, talked soothingly to the horse to ease her skittishness, and started down. He slack reined, allowing her to pick her way unguided down the steep grade. Far below a riderless horse wandered into view in the moonlight. His heart surged. Pickett getting around him, preceding him down, had descended into a box. Sheer walls rose on three sides, broken only by the trail he had descended. It looked as if a huge rectangular chunk of rock had been cut out like a piece of cake and lifted from the whole. The river churned by the open side of the box so rapidly that fording it, at least at this point, appeared impossible.

Raider dismounted and scrambled down the rest of the way on foot, bringing gravel clattering after him. He kept low, expecting lead to come his way at any second. As he

neared the bottom, he slowed. Pickett would be lying in
wait for him, he thought. He'd gun Raider down before he
could even catch sight of him.

Down he came to level ground, swinging his gun from
side to side, peering into the corners. The moment he
reached bottom, his right foot touching the rock-strewn
ground, there was a loud yell. Sweeping by, riding the
roaring river, came Pickett astride a log, vising it with his
legs, clutching a stunted branch with one hand and whipping the air with his hat with the other.

"Yeaaaaaa boyyyyyyy!"

For a split second Raider stood staring in shocked won-
derment, then brought up his gun and fired. But so fast was
the current moving, log, man, and hat swept past him and
were out of sight before he could hone in. He rushed forward into the water up to his knees, firing after the speed-
ing log and its occupant but missing cleanly.

Black with fury, he strode back up onto the shore, raised
his gun high, and brought it crashing down. It went off.
Raider jumped awkwardly. Startled by the shot, Pickett's
abandoned horse lunged forward, stopping just in time at
the water's edge. Raider's horse came ambling down to
join them.

CHAPTER SEVEN

Raider stood before the mirror over the washbowl surveying his likeness, which had been washed clean of his Indian makeup. He ran a finger over his naked upper lip and felt slightly sad. Was all this worth the loss of his mustache? Worth anything? He'd come so close to Mr. Stink. He could have had him, should have, only to lose him to the river.

Doc sat at the foot of the bed, tugging on an Old Virginia, watching him, listening to his recounting of his exploits.

"He's clever, Rade."

"He's bullshit. Reckless and lucky, that's what he is. I had him dead bang up in those hills when I was draped over the boulder. If he'd shown himself for just a split second . . . But no, he had to go sneakin' around those rocks and down outta there, down to below and find that log. Don't tell me that wasn't luck. Blind dumb luck. He knew he couldn'ta got across on his horse or leggin' it.

60

That current was movin' faster than falls, you betcha." He paused. "What am I tellin' you all this for? What do you have to know for? You and me are on the outs. I don't have to explain nothin' to a turncoat, a traitor. Cold-feet Weatherbee, that's you. I shouldn't even be talkin' to you."

"Are you quite through?"

"I shouldn't be!"

"Don't be ridiculous. You're lucky I threw in with Leroy. How would it look for Chicago to send reinforcements only to have the two of us turn our backs on them? Whether you like it or not, Rade, we're required to operate according to the *General Principles,* one of which clearly states that cooperation between and among operatives in the field is mandatory. The agency has no place for lone wolves."

"Tell me about it. I don't see as how you and Goldilocks did so great cooperatin'. I bet you fell on your faces. I don't hear you blowin' off your usual steam about that action out at the Patchett place. You musta screwed up for fair."

A knock at the door. It opened. Leroy Blodgett took one look at Raider and his handsome face fell, then tightened into an expression of virulent disdain.

"You're back, I see."

"With my tail between my legs? That what you wanta say? Say it. I dare ya."

"Oh, stop before you start, you two," rasped Doc. "I've already had it up to here with your ridiculous sniping. If you can't talk in a civilized manner to each other, don't talk at all. Come in, Leroy."

"Yeah, come in!" exclaimed Raider, glaring at Doc. "Come into my room. It's my room, too, Weatherbee. Come in and have tea and crumpets, Lee-roy."

"Shut up, Rade."

"Awwwwww..."

He finished toweling down. He had laid his buckskins out on the bed. Blodgett was staring at them.

"He went chasing after Ira Pickett, the ringleader, in that getup," explained Doc.

"How droll. Halloween. I take it you didn't catch him."

"He came within a whisker."

"I'll catch the son of a bitch, you betcha."

"Indeed? Far be it from me to throw cold water on any man's ambitions, but it behooves me to remind you of the *General Principles*. Chapter Four, paragraph C: under no circumstances shall a single operative—"

"All right, all right, nobody cares. Stick your *General Principles* up your—"

"Rade!"

"I gotta be bone stupid. I been chasin' around the territories for nearly twelve years in this dumb job and here I always figgered the idea was to catch the bastard, never mind how, when, or who, just grab him and bring him home."

"Leroy, if he feels he can accomplish more solo, accomplish something, I say we let him."

"*Let* me!" burst Raider. "How in hell either o' you gonna stop me?"

"Let him," continued Doc. "There's nothing in the rule book that says a man can't work undercover. Which in effect is what he's doing."

"Never mind me," said Raider. "Let's put the boot on the other foot. What you boys been up to lately? From the looks on your faces and the lack o' steam bein' blown off I'd say nothin' much. What happened out there at Patchett's? Spill it, I'm all ears. How many men you lose?"

A weariness deep-reaching and of considerable weight appeared to take hold of Blodgett. He sank slowly down onto the bed. He mumbled.

"I didn't hear ya. What'd he say?"

"Five dead, one badly wounded."

"Five! Holy jumpin'—"

"Take it easy, Rade, it was a rugged go, the worst I've seen in ages. We could easily have been wiped out completely."

"Five outta thirteen. A friggin' massacre."

"They lost more than that," said Doc.

"Big deal."

Blodgett had sunk into the doldrums, his elbows on his knees, his face propped on his palms. He shook his head slowly. "I'll never forgive myself for that boy."

"What boy?"

"Loyal Dressler, the recruit. Rade, it was very rough."

"Was it? Or did you boys make it rough? Whatja do, circle 'em, go at 'em in broad daylight?"

"Broad daylight, two in the morning, it wouldn't have made any difference," muttered Blodgett.

"It wouldn't have," said Doc. "Yes, we circled them. Unfortunately we had next to no cover. We tried to draw them out. We finally managed to."

He explained. Raider listened. He said nothing, only shook his head in obvious disapproval. Blodgett had raised his eyes and was watching him. Every time Raider shook his head Blodgett's face hardened more and his eyes further narrowed until by the time Doc was done they were slits.

"What else could we have done?" he burst out defensively.

Raider rubbed his jaw and furrowed his brow. "Your timin', like I said before. Just hold that in your heads. To start with you never should circle anyplace if you don't have the cover to cover yourselves with. All you do is make sittin' ducks o' yourselves, which you did, which proves my point."

"Rade . . ."

"Let me finish. Let me at least start. He asked what I woulda done—"

"He asked what else *we* could have done."

"Same thing. I woulda waited. I'm not talkin' for dark, since there wasn't any to speak of, I'm back talkin' time. Those boys inside were eatin' and drinkin' and playin' cards. They were blowin' off. They'd keep it up till midnight, maybe one o'clock, then fall asleep. Half of 'em would be stone drunk, the other half feelin' good enough to sleep through a friggin' thunderstorm, as good as out cold."

"Then what?" Doc asked.

"Then you make your move. Only not till then. A little patience always helps. You got thirteen men. You send nine out front positioned about a hundred fifty yards from the house spread out in a line. The other four approach from the rear, sneakin' up on the corral, which covers 'em, right? Now, let me take a minute here to talk about el'ments."

"Will you get on with it?" rasped Doc in exasperation.

"You got the corral, their horses, the distance from the back door—those are all el'ments. You put 'em to work for you. Help sharpen your edge. The nine out front give the four out back say three minutes. To do what? Sneak up to the corral, climb in, and hobble the horses. Even maybe tie one's foreleg to another's. I mean really hobble. Maybe even hobble the gate so they'll have to cut rope to get in.

"Okay, the three minutes are up. The boys out front open fire. Not a big barrage, just steady and 'nough to wake up them inside. What'll they do? They'll run to the front and fire back, right? When they start that, your attackers really open up, I'm talkin' throw everythin' but your boots at that place, blast and blast and blast. Pretty soon it'll get so hot them inside'll get discouraged."

"You hope."

"Hold the cold water, Doc. I heard you out, you hear me. They'll run to the back. It's like daylight out, they can see. They don't see a thing, not a sign of a soul, on accounta the four hobblers are all back to the far side o' the corral, hidin'. The coast is clear, they think. Out they come. They run to the horses. Hold your fire, give 'em a chance, and pretty soon all or at least most are come out the door. Then raise up and quicklike get the drop on 'em."

"You make it sound so easy," muttered Doc.

"Brilliant," said Blodgett.

"Maybe not, but it's gotta be better'n circlin' and lettin' 'em pick you off like grackles on a fence. You sure wouldn' lose any men, not if them out front stayed far 'nough back. And there'd be no need to come closer. The boys out back'd be handlin' the brunt of it. Damn, if I was only there, you'da come out of it without a scratch on any man, I betcha. Yeah, I sure shoulda been there. Them that got away never would have, not on hobbled horses they wouldn't. Right, Doc? Whatta ya think?"

"Mmmmmm . . ."

"Mmmm. That all you can say? Forget it, it's all over, over and blown for fair. Five dead."

"Will you stop saying that!" flared Blodgett.

"Five dead. So . . ." Raider sat down in the chair and slapped his knees. "Whatta ya got planned for tomorrow, another massacre?"

Blodgett shot to his feet and bulled forward, swinging. His left narrowly missed Raider's head. His right caught him in the cheek. Raider fell sideways out of the chair, sprawling on the floor, scrambling, jumping to his feet, sending a roundhouse at his attacker.

Doc was up, shoving between them. "Stop that! Stop it!"

He managed to keep each one at arm's length.

"The sucker punched me!" exclaimed Raider. "You saw! You come downstairs to the alley, coats off, sleeves up, and I'll beat you so, you goldy-locked son of a bitch, the shit'll be squeezin' outta your eyes!"

"I'll kill you!" growled Blodgett. "I'll close that big mouth forever!"

"Neither of you will do a damned thing. Now calm down. One more outburst and, so help me, I'll send a full report to the chief. I'll kick the two of you into the hottest soup of your lives."

"You'd do that, wouldn't you, Mr. Flasharity, turncoat, squeal on your partner, him who's saved your life maybe twenty-five or thirty times."

"Just shut up. And calm down. You too, Leroy. I know it would be absurd to ask either of you to shake hands and apologize, so we'll let that pass. Just no more fisticuffs or so help me I'll blow the whistle on you both."

"You got me all shakin' and sweatin' with worry," sneered Raider. He glared at Blodgett. "Whatta you hangin' around for? This here's our room. No visitors after ten o'clock. Take your conscience and get the hell out!"

Blodgett bristled and started for him.

Again Doc intervened. "Shut up, Rade, I mean it. You'd better go, Leroy."

He nodded and left.

The moment the door closed Doc turned on Raider. "You idiot! As if we didn't have our hands full enough without your petty picking, your stupid insults, your perpetual-motion mouth!"

"The sucker punched me."

"He should have broken your head. Rade, Rade, Rade, will you please at least try and get a handle on your temper with him? He'll try if you will, I know he will. This day's been a disaster for us. Losing those men shattered him, the boy especially. Did you have to rub salt in the wound? Does it warm you inside?"

"Yeah."

"I don't believe you. Nobody in his right mind is that malicious."

"Face it, we just don't like each other. Before this thing is wound up, we're gonna be at it like two cats in a barrel, you'll see. I never felt so about anybody else in my whole life like I do him. I'll break the son of a bitch into little pieces. That's what it's gotta come to. That's what it's gonna."

"No it isn't."

Raider glared and was about to disagree, but something in his partner's expression, in his eyes, gave him pause. He returned to the washbasin and began combing his hair.

CHAPTER EIGHT

Raider awoke in the morning with second thoughts—not about Leroy Blodgett, but about Ira Pickett. As Doc had said, Pickett was clever. A question crept into Raider's mind as he sat up in bed. It reared like a cobra. Had Pickett seen through his disguise after all? True, in all his bellowing and threatening he had called him redskin, bastard savage, and other uncomplimentary nicknames, but was it all purely for his benefit? Pickett knew the Pinkertons were after him. He knew Raider's build, his posture, his movements. He no doubt had an eye like an eagle to go along with his trail smarts. If he really took him for an Indian he'd hardly run away. Actually, he'd run from his Colt, and what Indian packed one? No, he may not have identified him as the sneezer in the express car, but he knew he was no Indian. And he knew too, or at least strongly suspected, that Raider was a Pinkerton.

Doc had awakened. Propped up on one elbow he studied his partner. "What are you doing?"

"Thinkin'."

"I can see that."

Raider's hand stole to the bruise on his cheek where Blodgett had hit him. "I'm gonna get back after Mr. Stink, Doc."

"We'll all be getting after him today."

"No way. He's mine. I've earned the son of a bitch."

"And what are we supposed to do, stand on the sidelines and cheer you on?"

"I don't care if you go rock huntin', just keep outta my way."

"Sorry, Rade, you had your lone-hand chance and blew it. This case belongs to all of us."

"All that's left."

"Don't start on that."

"Tell you what I'll do. You let me go my way, I let you and Goldilocks and your survivors go yours after them that got away from you last night. Maybe we'll bump into each other, maybe not. If we do we'll just say 'scuse me and move on. Besides them that got away you got prisoners. You said last night the marshall here in DeLamar wanted 'em outta his can quick as you could work it. You better get 'em outta there before he lets 'em out, before your friend Abington comes over and springs 'em. The marshal's doin' you a favor even takin' 'em in. He's got to live with Abington. He can stick his neck out just so far and no farther."

"Rade, if we mop this up properly, and we will, Abington will be finished. This case, with the trial to follow, will drag him and his nefarious career through the mud. The governor will come down on him so fast he won't have time to pack a bag. The only reason I can see that he's been able to keep it going this long is because Silver City's off in the middle of nowhere and has little or nothing to do with the smaller towns surrounding it. Boise's on the other side of the mountains. Nobody there cares what goes on in Owyhee County, least of all the governor, but when this thing breaks wide open you can start counting Abington's days."

"Maybe, but from where I sit you and Goldilocks got your hands full. Do yourselves a favor and leave Pickett to me."

"Are you going out as an Indian again?"

"Why not?"

"You don't look like one."

"Who says?"

"You don't hold yourself like one, walk or sit or move like one. You look like a white man on his way to a masquerade ball."

"You're fulla it. You're just jealous!"

"Of course. If only I had the guts to make a fool of myself."

"Shut up! Why don'tcha get up and get outta here. Go and have breakfast with your pal Goldilocks. You two go good together. Two peas same pod. Two college boys playin' at operativin'. You'll both be snickerin' outta the other side o' your mouths when I bring Mr. Stink in all trussed up like a turkey ready for the oven."

"Good luck."

"Shut up."

Raider ate breakfast alone in a diner at the far end of town to ensure steering clear of Doc, Blodgett, and the others. He had donned his disguise. He sat sipping his coffee and mulling over the situation. The last he'd seen of Ira Pickett was careening down the Snake River on the log. Once out of range he'd steered ashore, then no doubt circled around to come back after his horse. Raider had led it up the trail with his own and dropped both off at the livery stable.

Pickett would have no trouble getting another, but snatching his gave Raider a satisfying glow to go with his eggs and bacon. Small compensation for the hectic hours Pickett had put him through. Where would he go if he were Mr. Stink? Not back to Patchett's. Possibly into Silver City to powwow with his protector.

"He could be there this minute!"

The waitress, a scrawny relic with frizzy hair, beady eyes, and a mole on her chin, was staring at him. "Who could?"

"Nobody."

"You're no Indian."

"You figger that out all by yourself?"

"What are you doin' all dressed up like that?"

The door opened. In sailed Althea Mae, his verbal sparring partner from Grimshaw's Saloon and Gambling Emporium. She looked as if she hadn't slept in a week. Her pale face was drawn and haggard, her hair askew, exhaustion reddened her eyes, and mascara dripped from both lower lids. She stifled a yawn.

"Oh for Chrissakes, look what the cat dragged in."

"I asked what you're dressed up for," pressed the waitress.

"I heardja. None o' your beeswax. Ssssh, will ya!"

"Was there a party?" the waitress asked.

Althea Mae glided by, looking through him, corrugating her brow and, to his dismay, taking the seat beside him.

"Was there?"

Raider got up, fished out change, and laid it on the counter. The waitress continued to question him. Althea followed him to the front with her bleary eyes. He was halfway out the door when she recognizd him.

"Hey you. You! Foulmouth! I'm talking to you!"

He closed the door behind him. Her shrill voice rattled the glass.

"Fatass," he muttered.

He walked two doors up the street and leaned against one of the six uprights supporting the overhang of Nieman's Haberdashery. Yes, Pickett would definitely run back to Silver City. Where else could he find a decent bed?

Raider walked back to the livery stable and got out his horse and Pickett's. He rode east toward Silver City, leading the outlaw's mount.

•   •   •

The morning was brutally bright, the sun already searing the desiccated landscape. Raider was sweating. He could feel his makeup striping his forehead and cheeks and was tempted to wipe his face clean. Barging into town looking exactly as he'd looked the night before wasn't the smartest move to make. He might just as well follow a brass band in. If Pickett spotted him first he'd recognize him in a second and likely run for the hills.

He hobbled both horses behind Kleck's Union Market. He sneaked back to the rear of the sheriff's office and, mounting the steps, leaned over the railing as far as he could and sneaked a peek through the barred window. The cells were empty, but the inner door stood wide open, and through it he could see Abington's broad back. He was seated at his desk talking to somebody. Whoever it was, all Raider could see were his pantlegs and well-scuffed boots. They showed a much deeper scallop top than his own, and the heels were well set under. He hadn't noticed what Pickett was wearing, hadn't gotten close enough to see, and probably wouldn't have observed them if he had. The two men seemed to be carrying on like two old socks, Abington laughing and slapping his knee every so often. Once he reached for a packet of shag tobacco in a desk drawer and crammed a handful into his mouth. Then the other man leaned across to get some for himself. Leaned squarely into view.

"Pay dirt! Hot dog!"

Raider went back to the horses, loosened their hobbles, and led them down through the backyards and into the first alley he came to. Moving through it, he crossed the street and went down the alley opposite. He walked them back the other way and stood looking down the side of the building. He had a clear view of the office front door. Grass flourished in the yard behind him; he left the horses to feed, looking back at then every now and then to make sure neither wandered.

He waited an hour, eyes riveted to the door. He could

see Abington clearly through the right front window, but the door blocked his view of Pickett. He was not worried that the outlaw might leave by the back way. If he did so, Abington would get up, signaling the move. Maybe wouldn't get up, but would at least turn in his chair or even just turn his head. But he didn't turn and didn't budge from the chair.

His impatience mounting by the minute, Raider fidgeted and fumed. Sweat had ruined his makeup. He had no mirror, but he could picture it running down his face, leaving his cheeks all smeared. He finally got out his bandanna and wiped and wiped until the cloth was a solid brown. To hell with the disguise. It was getting close to man-to-man, there'd be no need to hide his identity when the chasing started and the guns came out.

He waited into the second hour; in all that time neither man had stirred. They talked and talked and talked.

"They're worse'n two old maids."

He was tempted to cross the street, barge in gun in hand, and take Pickett. Lock Abington in one of his cells and get out. But headstrong heroics always seemed to get messy in a hurry. Somebody could interfere. Abington would raise a big fuss, bringing his deputies running, or Raider and his prisoner could bump into some of Pickett's friends before they got to the end of the street and into the clear.

No, better to continue waiting until Pickett left, no matter how long it took. Let him get on his horse and leave. The lonesome-looking sorrel out front with the California-Oregon saddle had to be his.

Raider fretted and waited. He was beginning to feel hungry when the front door finally opened two inches. And stopped there, no doubt with Abington's hand on the knob while he finished what he was saying.

"Come on, damn it!"

Raider ran back to the horses and quickly hobbled the one he'd taken from Pickett the night before. Then he returned to his post. Both men came out jawing and chew-

ing. The sheriff walked him to his horse. Pickett unhitched
and got on. Raider mounted and rode parallel with him
through the backyards until the buildings gave out. He then
fell in behind him well behind his dust. Pickett headed for
DeLamar. His two men that Doc and Blodgett had taken
prisoner would still be in jail there. What was he going to
do, try and break them out? Had Abington refused to lend
him a hand? It didn't appear so when Pickett left him.
They had parted with smiles on both their faces and a great
show of fellowship.

On Pickett cantered, Raider following. DeLamar came
into view, but the moment Raider spotted it Pickett's dust
turned off the road in the direction of the Owyhees.

"Good! Great! Now I gotcha!"

Once up into the mountains Raider closed the gap between himself and his quarry, thanks to the myriad convo-
lutions of the trail and the concealment afforded by the
rocks at every turn. Some were gigantic, as tall as five-
story buildings. There was little vegetation—only clumps
of grass clinging tenaciously to life here and there and an
occasional stunted pine or scrub oak. Pickett seemed to be
heading for the summit. There Raider would catch up with
him and have it out, he decided. He had no heart for a
repeat of the night before and the almost sheer descent
down the far side to the river where he'd lost him. Happily,
Pickett seemed inclined to cooperate. Nearing the top, he
turned off the trail, riding a narrow path across the face of
an inclined plane of bare rock and out of sight. Raider
started to follow, then changed his mind and climbed
higher before crossing over.

In time he reached a spot just above where Pickett had
vanished from sight. Looking down he could see a flat
open area roughly shaped like a flatiron, one end cut
square across, the other coming to a point. A small shack
with a corrugated iron roof occupied one side, the materials
for it evidently mule-packed up the slopes. Pickett had left
his horse to graze on the grass surrounding the shack and

looked to be getting ready to build a fire.

Raider dismounted and looked straight down at him bent over the ash pit circled by small rocks. Pickett's back presented an inviting target; had he been so inclined he could have killed him then and there with one shot, but he'd never back-shot a man in his life and was not about to start now. Besides, he was much more valuable alive.

He thought a moment. If he called down to him, ordered him to freeze, knowing him, he wouldn't. He'd draw and whirl at the same time and get off at least one shot. Raider would have to kill him then.

Somehow Raider had to outfox him. If he could only sneak down without his seeing him, down behind the shack, come around the side, and get the drop on him, he could easily take him without a shot. But getting down without being seen or heard, without sending down a shower of pebbles to announce his coming, appeared impossible.

If he called to him, ordering him to freeze, he might not draw and fire. He might whirl around and jump through the doorway less than four feet behind him. If he got inside, Raider would never get him out without climbing down and confronting him. Pickett was no fool. He might very well let Raider come down without a fight, only to open up when he got close.

How to get close enough to catch him by surprise, get the drop on him, and collar him without a shot? He might be able to do it under cover of darkness, but night was a good eight hours away, and even when it did arrive it would probably be as bright as the night before.

He drew back out of sight, squatted on his haunches, and thought about it. And came to the conclusion that attempting any move from this position, almost directly over Pickett's head a good fifty feet up, was out of the question. He'd be far better off circling wide and getting back down to the narrow trail that led into the rocks, the open area, and the shack. Approach him on foot and surprise him at eye level.

He found a wide way back down, left his horse at the head of the path banding the face of the rock, and, gun in hand, started across. When he came within sight of the open space and the shack Pickett was nowhere to be seen. His sorrel stood nibbling grass, swishing her tail contentedly, the saddle still on her back. The fire had not yet been started.

Pickett was inside the shack. Raider cocked his head, aimed, and strained one ear at the open doorway, but could hear nothing. His gun ready, he started toward it, picking his way through the grass as quietly as he could, coming up to the open door. He nimbly stepped to the right and looked in, then to the other side and did the same.

The shack was empty.

"Lookin' for me, Pink?" Raider froze. Pickett laughed. "Drop it and reach."

He obeyed.

"Turn around." At Pickett's feet was scattered firewood, dropped when he'd pulled his gun.

"Jumpin' javalinas!" He began laughing uproariously. "Whatja do to your face? It's all smeared. Who you supposed to be, Chief Washakie? Ya look more like a medicine show getup artist, the one that beats the tom-tom when the pitchman starts shoveling the crap about his snake oil. Man, you look dumb!"

"Why don'tcha cut the chin wagglin' and give it up?"

"Whadda ya talkin' about? I'm holdin' the gun." He sucked in his breath sharply and sneezed. "Son of a bitch! I got a cold. Caught it from you in that express car down by Thunder Mountain. You sneezed square in my face and gave it to me."

"I don't remember."

"You did so, you careless slob!"

"Can I lower my hands?"

"Hell no. You might as well die with 'em up as down."

"What do you wanta shoot me for?"

"Whaja wanta shoot me?"

"I didn't. I don't. I coulda easy when I was up top. I

coulda drilled you down between the shoulders when you were bendin' over the fire."

"You shoulda. It was your last chance."

"You're done for, Ira."

He seemed surprised that Raider knew his name. "What's your name?"

"Raider. Phew, man do you stink!"

"What are you sayin' a insultin' thing like that for?"

"It's the bald truth. Christ Almighty, don't you ever take a bath? You smell like a barn fulla dead rats."

"I smell fine to me. You ain't exactly a bouquet o' roses."

"I don't stink. You stink."

"Shut up. You're a Pinkerton, ain'tcha?"

"Hell no, whatever give you that idea? You are finished, though, whether you realize it or not. Your boys are killed, jailed, or scattered. You're all by your lonesome. Why don'tcha wise up, fold your deuces, and come back to Elko with me quiet-like? I'll see you get a fair shake."

"You'll see I get a rope, and you're wrong about my boys. My two sons are still around, and my friends Asa Hudlin and Willis McColl. They'll take care o' your sidekick if they ain't already, and what's left o' that bunch that come to help you. You're the one's finished."

"You're no spring chicken. You can't keep runnin' forever."

"Who the hell's runnin'? You see me runnin'? You got it all twisted up."

"You screwed up for fair back at Thunder Mountain, you know. You blew it. You held up for a lousy six hundred bucks, rode away, and left half a million in silver in the mail car."

"You're a damn liar!"

"It's the gospel truth."

Pickett eyed him. Malevolence came creeping into his narrowed eyes. "I oughta blow your ears off for starters just for tellin' me that. You like to stick the needle in, don'tcha? You enjoy it."

"Just tellin' you the true facts."

"Shut up, I'm thinkin'."

"Be smart, give me your iron."

"Shut up or I'll give ya lead, damn ya." He furrowed his face in thought, then brightened. "We're leavin'. We're goin' over and join Asa, Willis, and the boys. I'm takin' you along and keepin' you alive. For a spell. You're gonna come in handy. You're gonna be our tradin' hostage for my two men sittin' in jail in DeLamar. I'm gonna swap you one for two, and if your partner and the marshal refuses me, then I'll kill ya. If you're not worth tradin' for, you're not worth keepin' alive. Right? Right!"

Again he sneezed. Raider laughed. Pickett glared.

CHAPTER NINE

Pickett relieved Raider of his belt along with his gun and tied his hands behind his back, slipping a stick behind him and through his crooked elbows "just to keep ya' comfor'ble." They rode down out of the Owyhees between De-Lamar and Silver City toward the Nevada border. Along the way Pickett regaled him with tales of his more recent exploits, interspersed with lavish praise for his two boys, Jason and Caleb. He made them sound like two heroes of the Indian wars, sterling characters, pillars of virtue, paragons of courage, when in reality they were as low, cowardly, and villainous as their father. Raider was sorely tempted to interrupt and tell him so, but it would only beg a bullet in the face, he decided, and held his peace.

They forded Boulder Creek and came onto the Summit Plateau. Pickett stopped them. "Whadja do with my horse?"

"It's back in Silver City waitin' for me."

"It's got a long wait. You got some gall, stealin' a man's horse."

"You stole it first."

"I did like hell. I bought it from a fella, gear and all. Paid him cash money." He eyed Raider evilly. "Pinkerton, before I get through with you you're gonna rue the day you ever started chasin' me. I promise you will. What I'd really like to do, what'd be perfect would be to swap you, get clear, circle round, come back, and kill ya. That'd be ideal, and that's what I'll end up doin', watch me."

"If you were as big as your mouth you'd need a damn elephant to carry you."

"You're temptin' me . . ." He started to add more, then stopped abruptly. "What's that?"

"What?"

"Riders." He turned about and shaded his eyes from the sun. "Oh, Jesus."

Indians. At first glance at least thirty, probably a Shoshone hunting party. This was their territory, actually close to the heart of it. Raider's heart sank, then just as quickly lifted. Better they both be captured by them than he by Mr. Stink.

Up they barreled, quickly surrounding them. They were Shoshones, no mistaking their garb, identical to Raider's own. The leader wore a black high-domed derby with a single eagle feather sticking straight up out of the brim. He looked ridiculous. But Raider looked even more ridiculous to him. He took one look, pointed, and began roaring. The others joined in. Loud guffawing circled Pickett and his prisoner.

"*Sho sho gala, atha gala!*" burst Black Derby. He mimed smearing his face with his hand derisively.

"He thinks you're a riot," said Pickett, leering.

"Shut up. Go back to your sneezin', why don'tcha."

Pickett obliged him and glared. "You savvy their lingo?"

"Hell no."

"So hand-talk the sons o' bitches. Tell Mr. Hat we're peaceful and good friends o' their tribe. Tell him we hate the Blackfoot and the Crow. Tell him we just wanta go on our peaceful way without no trouble. Tell him—"

"Tell him, tell him, tell him yourself, goddamn it!"

"You do like I say, Raider, or I'll plug you right in front of 'em. They don't care what I do with ya."

"How'm I supposed to sign with my damn hands tied, you asshole!"

Pickett hesitated, studied Black Derby, then quickly untied Raider. "Do it!"

Raider grunted and held up his right hand, knuckles forward, thumb alongside, sweeping it down indicating "bad," at the same time nodding at Pickett. He then swept his hand toward his chest, indicating he was taking him in.

"Whatja say?"

"That you're a great chief."

"Bullshit!"

Black Derby barked an order. Pickett was speedily relieved of his gun and Raider's and both were ordered to move out.

"You screwed up, Pink, you didn't tell him what I tolja. We're sunk now, and it's all your fault. I'll get you for this!"

"You stink."

Arriving at the Indians' campsite, they were pushed into a tepee. Raider sat and finished wiping off the rest of his makeup.

Pickett stared fixedly at him. "This is some nice mess you've got us into. I oughta beat you to death!"

"Let's see you try. I'll bust ya into bird feed!"

"Ha, that'll be the day." He sniffed and made a face. "This place stinks."

"How would you know?"

"Shut up."

An idea crawled into Raider's head. "Hey!"

"What?"

"You know about Shoshones?"

"Course." There was a pause. "What about 'em?"

"They got this ceremonial rite, what they call the blood altar."

"What's that?"

"They get a big stone, and a certain time o' the year, before the harvest, along about now, they make themselves a blood sacrifice. So the harvest'll turn out good, you know? They offer up gourds fulla human blood to the Great Spirit. Captives' blood. White-eyes' blood."

Pickett gaped. "Ours?"

"Bet your boots. Why else grab us this time o' year? You know the Shoshones, they're peaceful as the Hopis. Been gettin' along with the white man ever since Colonel Augur give 'em Wind River Valley for their own back in '68."

"This ain't the Wind River Valley."

"It's the neighborhood. What I'm gettin' at is because they're peaceful they're left pretty much to themselves, to do what they want, live like their ancestors. You made a big mistake, Ira, trespassin' on ther sacred land."

"How'm I supposed to know this is theirs?"

"You gotta be careful where you stray in this corner o' the territory."

"You knew. Whyn'cha say somethin'?"

"Hell, you'd only've accused me o' lyin'. Still, I shoulda. We wouldn't be in this fix now."

"We gotta get outta here, Pink. I don't wanta end up fillin' up gourds and pots for no harvest altar or whatever it is."

"Blood altar."

"We gotta get away. You think we can?"

"Maybe, if we can hold out till dark. Course there's no tellin' when they'll come for us to tie us to the poles and cut our hearts out."

"What?"

"That's the first part o' the sacrifice."

"Jesus."

"It's generally done in the mornin' when the sun's low. Then when it gets up to the top o' the sky they bury the hearts, fill the gourds with blood, and make their prayers to the Great Spirit. It's quite a show, they say."

"Yeah, yeah. Look, let's you and me call a truce, work together and get outta here, whatta ya say?"

"A truce?"

"I promise faithfully, cross my heart hope to die, I won't lay a hand on ya if you'll throw in with me so's we can get us both outta here and away from these here blood-thirsty bastards."

"A truce."

"Deal?"

"You know I trust you about as far as I can throw my horse."

"I just give you my solemn word o' honor!"

"I guess you're right, we got no choice but to work together. But we can't do a thing till dark. And you better cross your fingers and pray it's darker than last night. If it's not we won't get ten feet." Raider got up and began inspecting the hide wall.

"What are you doin'?"

"This is old and dried out. I can practically cut it with my fingernail. Belt buckle prong'll do fine. What are you doin'?"

"Prayin' for cloud cover, for pitch black dark!"

Pickett showed Raider the $600 stolen from the express car, that is to say, $578 of it. Having joined forces with him, he had shed his ornery crust and become amiable, as comradely as he'd been with Nat Abington in the office earlier. Raider wanted to ask him about Abington, how long he and his gang had been under his protection, how it worked, what Abington charged for his "services," but it wasn't important. He laughed inwardly. Pickett had swallowed his blood altar story hook, line, sinker, and pole. Fear had surfaced in his eyes as he listened to Raider detail what they were in for if they didn't get away. He may have been an experienced high-line rider, but he sure didn't know Indians. As far as that went, few outlaws did; they had no need to, they had little or nothing to do with the tribes. If Pickett only knew the truth. The Shoshones had been nothing but peaceful toward the white man since Lewis and Clark enlisted their help on their famous expedition. Sacagawea, the squaw who had accompanied them, was a Shoshone.

As the shadows lengthened and Pickett grew more worried about his immediate future, food—dried buffalo meat, corn, and water—was brought to them. Knowing the Shoshone as he did, Raider found himself wondering why they had captured them and brought them to camp in the first place. They certainly didn't intend to kill them; they spilled Blackfoot and Crow blood, not white men's. What were they cooking up for them? He snickered. He didn't plan to stick around long enough to find out. Out he'd get and take Pickett with him.

Then what? They'd be on foot without so much as a penknife between them. Toe to toe he could probably take Pickett, but he mustn't discount the obvious. Pickett was tough as a goat, and no doubt handy with his fists. He looked tough, acted tough, and likely was, and if it came to a battle royal between them, he'd have only one edge: he'd be fighting for his life.

Doc agreed with Leroy Blodgett that it would be a waste of time to go back to the Patchett house after the outlaws who had fled from there the night before. It would be pointless for them to return. The problem as Doc saw it was that they had no idea what the outlaws looked like, having only seen them fleetingly when they rode away. On second thought, he and Raider *had* seen them—three of them in the express car with Pickett.

Raider. He appeared to be the lucky one; he could spot Pickett from two hundred yards away. If and when he got on his trail again he'd very likely catch up with him and take him. Blodgett suggested they leave the men and the two of them ride into Silver City and nose about separately. Doc wasn't keen on the idea. One or the other or both

might be recognized and caught in the middle of the outlaws' stamping grounds. Easy prey. Too easy.

The situation was becoming increasingly frustrating
until Doc came up with an admittedly rash idea, but one he
liked. Everyone had mounted up in front of the Bluebird
preparatory to riding out. Doc took off his derby and
scratched his head, suggesting that he was bringing his idea
to the surface.

Blodgett could see his wheels turning. "Say it."

"Well, to begin with, what are we kidding ourselves
for? We know the ones we're after and Pickett's sons and
his two close friends are somewhere in Silver City. Nat
Abington's probably squirreled them away and will keep
them there till we've cleared out. I see him as the key."

"He's not the one we're after."

"But he's the kingpin. Indulge me, Leroy. If we removed him from the picture everybody under his protection, including those we're after, wouldn't be inclined to
hang around. They wouldn't feel safe. They'd get out.
Wouldn't you?"

"I see what you mean, and I agree."

"Good."

"But we have no authority to arrest Abington."

"Let's not split hairs. The man's guilty of obstructing
justice. On a dozen counts. A hundred. If you're worried
about protocol, we can get an arrest order from Judge Aldergate."

"Who's he?"

"*The* judge in Silver City, according to my young
friend, Joshua Kincaide, the photographer."

"What makes you think he'll give you one? If he's *the*
judge in town, why hasn't he done something with Abington before this?"

"He's reputedly wishy-washy, as is the mayor, but—"

"Doc, I think you're barking up the wrong tree. Abington's not our concern."

"But he is! The more I think about it the more I wonder
why we haven't concentrated on him from the start. He

should be arrested, whisked out of town to . . . to Boise, locked up, and then just watch the rats desert the ship. I'll tell you what. I'll go into town, walk into his office, and herd him out the back door at gunpoint. I'll take a couple of men with me and ride over the mountains straight for Boise. It's no more than seventy miles. While we're gone you cover both ways out of town, east and west." He began to describe the three men who entered the express car with Ira Pickett.

Blodgett waved him to a stop. "No, Doc. Forget it. I'm asking you to, and I'm in charge."

"Why not?"

"Too complicated. It'll never work. You're forgetting his deputies. They'll rally round him, and there could be a bloody fracas before we even get close to the ones we want. In two minutes flat we'd have every outlaw in town against us. He's probably got a hundred under his wing. You think they're going to let their meal ticket be snatched out from under their noses without a fight? It'd be suicide."

"Abington's the key!"

"No! Don't you understand English?"

"You're ridiculous, you know that? Raider's right, you're insufferable."

"No need for sniping, Weatherbee. Men, here's what we do, we'll ride an ever-widening circle around Silver City, and with any luck at all we should run into the ones that got away. When we do, we'll try to take them without a shot."

"You're not ridiculous!" boomed Doc. "You're a blithering idiot!"

So saying, he heeled his horse and galloped away. Blodgett called after him threateningly. Doc never looked back.

When darkness fell, and before Raider and Pickett could make a move, they had a visitor, Komoso, Little Eagle, the chief. He looked close to a hundred, his face as wrinkled as a walnut and the identical color, his body shrunken, twisted, and riddled with arthritis from the look of him. In he came with Black Derby. To the surprise of both prisoners Little Eagle spoke English.

"You dress like Shoshone?" he pointedly asked Raider.

"To catch this son of a bitch."

"Son of—"

"Chief, this man's my prisoner, I was takin' him in."

"Don't listen to him, Chief!" burst Pickett. "He's lyin' in his store teeth. He's *my* prisoner. Tell him, Derby Hat, when you come up, who was tied up? Wasn't me, it was him. I'm a Pinkerton detective, he's a train robber, and I'm takin' him in. If you boys know what's good for you, if you don't want the Duck Valley agent comin' down on you like a avalanche you'll drop all this bullshit here and now and let us go, let me take him in like it's my sworn duty to!"

"Why don't you shut your stupid trap!" bawled Raider. "Your mouth makes me sicker than your stink, you bowlegged bastard."

Black Derby jerked out a knife ten inches long, waving it between them. "No more talk!"

"No more!" exclaimed the chief. "I speak. You whiteeyes are not our enemies. We have lived in peace with you ever since the days of Washakie. Our enemy is the Crow." He pointed toward the opening. "Chief Medicine Crow has captured four of our braves. He has sent us word that they will be sacrificed if we not give up four of his braves captured hunting."

"So trade him!" burst Pickett. "Even up swap. Whatta ya want with us?"

"We trade for our warriors."

"I hate to say he's right," said Raider, "but he is."

The chief stopped him with his hand. He talked briefly to Black Derby.

"It's dumb," added Raider.

The chief shook his head. "It is only way. Sheriff in Twin Falls holds two Crow braves in cells for murder of white trapper. Crows need you to trade for them."

"Bullshit!" snapped Pickett.

"The white sheriff won't do it," said Raider. "That's not the way sheriffs operate. You're barkin' up the wrong tree in the wrong woods. We'd like to lend ya a hand if we could, but what you're sayin' just won't work."

Little Eagle lifted one withered and twisted finger. He pointed first to Pickett, then to Raider. "We trade you."

This said he got up and walked out. Black Derby lingered. He seemed suddenly angry. Again he flashed his knife. *"Lacco o mana komi. Lacco amta!"*

"Get lost," sneered Pickett.

To Raider's mild surprise he left.

"We gotta get outta here pronto," said Pickett.

"In a bit." Raider went to the flap and peered out. "There's a little cloud cover, but not much. We'll give it another half hour or so. Let it get dark as it's gonna, keep watch, and see when the biggest cloud starts across the moon. Then make a run for it."

"Let's go now."

"Don't be such a yellowbelly. With the chips down you got no more balls than a fish!"

Pickett growled and swung. Raider ducked just in time. He could feel Pickett's fist breezing over the part in his hair.

"Watch it, Mr. Stink, you try that again and I'll leave you here. You need me. We got a deal, you and me."

Again Pickett growled. "Quit muddin' me, I don't like it!"

Their shared plight could not help but forge something of a bond between them, the frequent eruptions of animosity notwithstanding. Raider would never openly admit it, but in his heart he knew that Pickett was cut from the same rough bolt of cloth as he. How they could end up on opposite sides of the fence struck him as odd.

"Where you come from 'riginally?" he asked.

"Mississippi. You?"

"Arkansas."

"Arkansas razorback hog. Ha. Ugliest critter in America. Your pappy farm?"

"My pa died, stepfather farmed. Tried to. Wasn't much good at it."

"Was the soil, I betcha. We had us a farm. Near James in Washington County. Fifty acres. Tried to grow cotton, beans, couldn't grow neither, not 'nough to fill a horse trough. Couldn't grow shit. Too many rocks, too much sand in the soil. We like to starve, near did. Ma, Pappy, me, and Orland, and my sister Rose o' Sharon Elsie. Never once't had us a decent crop o' neither. Growed weeds, they come up great. Then we lost it all."

"The bank?"

"River. One spring, '54, '55, I can't 'member, she overflowed, busted her banks from Friar's Point clear down to Vidalia. Flood like you wouldn't believe. Water come clear up to the second-story windows. We had to climb out up onto the roof. Sat there all five o' us in the drivin' rain. Come mornin' that water surgin' round us scary as hell picked up that old house and off we sailed, spinnin' and turnin' . . . Rose o' Sharon Elsie screamin', Ma hollerin', Pappy cursin' blue. We coulda drowned for fair. Was still rainin' buckets, barrels, like it was never goin' to stop."

"What happened?"

"We got washed downstream for better'n five mile before bumpin' into a magnolia stump big as a cowshed, snaggin' onto it. It drove clean through the front door and out the back, wrecked that old house practically into kindlin'. There we sat till dark, water swirlin' round, not 'nother livin' soul in sight. We was beginnin' to think we was the only survivors in the whole state, maybe the whole South. Sat shiverin' through the whole next night. When the sun come up the rain had let up and the water was droppin' fast.

"We all lived through it, but it was the end o' farmin' for Pappy. Him and Ma went to the poorhouse in Greenville, and us kids scattered. Rose o' Sharon Elsie went to live with Aunt Ola and Uncle Anson in Louisiana. Me and Orland just cut out. I was twelve."

"You stole a gun and went to work."

"I stole nothin'. I went to work river-bargin'. Toughest job in Christendom. Made me hard like a rock. Bet you never done a hard day's work in your life."

"Oh hell no, I've had it soft as a kitten since the farm. I been livin' in clover, women, champagne."

"How'd you ever get into the Pinkertons o' all things?"

"Oh, that was harder'n hell. I hadda sign my name and everything."

"Why?"

"Why what?"

"Why'dja ever wanta take up a job snitchin' and double-crossin' folks? A Pinkerton's got to be the most hateful job there is, worse'n a hangman."

"Do tell."

"Wrenchin' husbands outta their women's arms, away from their little ones, lockin' people up, pushin' 'em into court, gettin' 'em hunged and the firin' squad, torture . . . God Almighty, you must have one helluva time sleepin' nights. I'll bet you don't. I'll bet your conscience beats you to death. Or ain'tcha got none?"

"Course not, what would I do with a conscience?"

"I'm serious. Man, you must be some embarrassment to your kin, holdin' down such a shameful job o' work. You must hide your face in your hat every time you bump into somebody you know from the old days."

"You're fulla shit, you know that? You gotta be the biggest little lowlife I come across in ten years and you sit there the pot callin' the kettle black, criticizin' me, a law-'bidin' citizen."

"You're a legal skunk, that's what you are. Still, I expect you can't help it, it's a weakness in your blood you got from your folks. My folks was church people; my grandpappy was a stump preacher. Traveled all over savin' souls, pullin' folks back from the door to hell, rescuin' 'em from damnation."

"He missed out on you, right?"

"Whatcha talkin' about, I'm no sinner."

"Oh hell no."

"I ain't!"

"You murder, you rob, rape, and rustle. You'd steal the pennies off a dead man's eyes, the nickels from a blind man's cup, dimes from the church poor box. They could hang you ten times over it wouldn't come near payin' for your crimes. You must be proud o' yourself. Your sons must be proud o' you."

"Proud and respect me, look up to me."

"Bet you taught 'em everything they know 'bout crime."

"Never teached 'em nothin', 'cept how to use a gun. Every man should know how to use a gun. It's a dangerous world we live in, harsh and unrewardin'. You only get what you take; nobody gives nothin'. That's somethin' else I teached 'em. Everythin' else they learnt is self-taught. They look up to me like good sons should. What else should they do but folly in my footsteps?"

"Has it ever crossed your mind you could be plowin' the wrong furrow? Followin' the straight and narrow might give you a better life? You and them?"

"I tried it; didn't work. I couldn't make it. You ever think o' tryin' it?"

"It's gettin' dark. Time we stirred our stumps."

It was nearly two hours before Doc simmered down and was able to resume thinking straight. He had wandered about DeLamar fuming, talking to himself, attracting the stares of passersby, feeling his cheeks tingle in embarrassment. He decided his best course would be to try and find Raider; he certainly hadn't left the area. Was he still in disguise? Hopefully not. Was he in Silver City? Probably not, not unless Ira Pickett was. Prying Mr. Stink, his sons, and his sidekicks loose from their safe harbor promised a considerable chore. If Raider was there and working on it he could use help.

On the way over another idea came to him, one he should have brought to mind the day before or even earlier. Joshua Kincaide had come over to DeLamar with the telegram from Chicago. They had talked while Raider ate breakfast. When the photographer left he'd mentioned off-handedly that Pickett and his brood were scheduled to have their picture taken. Doc recalled asking him to develop an extra set of prints for him.

First things first. Upon arriving in Silver City he would go straight to Kincaide's. He rode into town at a lope, passing Hurtlemeyer's Cash Store and the sheriff's office, noting the batch of wanted dodgers out front, Abington's private little joke on the decent people in town, his way of rubbing their noses in it.

He hitched in front of Kincaide's house, and when he knocked, Joshua let him in. He was in vest and shirt-sleeves, evidently hard at work. To Doc's surprise and some disappointment he didn't seem at all pleased to see him again.

"I'm up to my ears," he began.

"I won't take long. I just wanted a word."

He closed the door and Doc followed him into the studio.

"Alvina's gone over to Gooding to visit her cousin, I'm batching it for a few days. What can I do for you?"

"Did you make an extra set of prints of Pickett and his sons for me?"

He got them out. There were five in all, eight-by-tens unframed. All five outlaws—Pickett, his boys, and his two friends—posed in two pictures, displaying their artillary and their grins for posterity. Pickett looked like a hairy bantam rooster. There was a shot of him and his two boys, another of him, Hudlin, and McColl, and the last of him alone.

Doc got out his wallet. Joshua shook his head and showed his palm vertically. "No charge." He shifted his eyes, looking over his visitor's shoulder at the front door.

"Can I steal a couple more minutes?" Doc asked.

"Of course. Won't you sit down? I made coffee, but I'm afraid it's cold."

"Thank you no. Joshua, you've been very helpful, don't think it isn't appreciated. Frankly, you're our only contact here, you and Mrs. Kincaide, the only people we dare trust." His listener's expression said "get to the point." Doc did so. "We—that is, my partner and I—when we hook up we're going after Abington. I see him as the key to this case."

He had expected Joshua's face to light up with this revelation. To his surprise it had the opposite effect. Undaunted, he continued.

"If you think about it, removing him from the scene would be as helpful as collaring Pickett and his sons, and could make it a lot easier. With him out of the way most of the outlaws under his wing will scatter. In a matter of hours normalcy would be restored."

"If you're telling me this for my opinion, I have to say I don't think it's a very good idea."

"Oh?"

Joshua went to first one window looking out on the street, then the other, and pulled the shades. He then went to the door and locked it.

"You came here to catch Pickett. Shouldn't you continue to concentrate on him until you do? Isn't he the sole reason why you came here in the first place?"

"But . . ."

"Mr. Weatherbee."

"Doc."

Joshua sighed heavily and dropped down onto a stool, his hands clapping his knees. "There's something I have to tell you. We townspeople are getting ready to take matters into our hands. We're going after Abington tonight. We're more than forty strong."

"I wouldn't do it, Josh, you'll be making a big mistake."

"We don't think so. We should have done it six years

ago. We'll be doing it tonight." He half laughed grimly. "Better late then never, eh?"

"What does Alvina think? Or doesn't she know?"

"As I said, there's no charge for the prints. I wish you luck. I hope they come in handy. I hope you'll be able to hook up with your partner and collect Ira and the others."

"Joshua . . ."

"It's our problem, Doc."

"It could easily turn into a bloodbath. You won't be going up against just him and his deputies, there's the rotten element he's cozy with. They'll side with him, they'll fight for him. You'll have your hands full."

"We know, we've talked it to death. Nothing can happen that we won't expect, but it's now or never. Let me explain something, an angle to it that you who don't live here probably haven't thought about. The decent people in this town, people who were here long before this thing started, feel like . . . like prisoners, like a people conquered by an invader, obliged to live and work and bring up their children in shadow if you will. Abington and his hold on us are like a disease. It infects everyone. You can't walk down the street, can't walk into a store and buy something without seeing his rabble. Have you any idea how that makes us feel, how helpless, put upon, knowing he's virtually in charge of our very lives, and laughing at us?

"It makes a man feel gelded! I do. I'm ashamed to look Alvina in the eye. Oh, she doesn't say anything, she wouldn't, but there's something in her eyes, they're . . . accusing."

"You can see it."

"I do."

"You imagine you do, but it's not there."

"It is. Every time that man smiles at me I feel castrated. He's got to go. This disease has got to be stamped out for good. We've got to take back our town, and if he has to die, if some of us do, so be it."

"Josh, I understand, I do, and I sympathize with you,

but you don't know what you're letting yourselves in for. They outnumber your valiant forty better than two to one, they're professionals, they can shoot a man as easily as you flick lint from your sleeve. Can you? Can any of you? You think you can, you're angry enough to, but when the time comes . . ."

"There's really no point in our discussing it. It's our problem, and we intend to deal with it. Finally. It's nice to see you again. Now . . ."

Doc shrugged. It was all that came to mind. There was nothing further he could say, nothing Kincaide would listen to. He tucked the envelope containing the photographs under his arm and left.

Raider and Pickett got a shock just before they broke out of the tepee, which Raider promptly turned into a break. While Pickett watched the biggest cloud in the deep-blue heavens slide across the face of the moon, plunging the camp into pitch darkness, Raider started ripping the hide wall opposite the entrance flap. Pickett came over to him—almost immediately followed by Black Derby. Raider caught the sound of the sub-chief entering. Black Derby started, gaping blankly, then went for his knife. Raider dove past Pickett, tackling the Shoshone around the lower legs and downing him.

Pickett raised one leg and brought his boot crashing down on the Indian's face, knocking him cold.

"What the hell did you do that for?" Raider rasped, retrieving the knife.

"He's out, ain't he? It's what you wanted, ain't it?"

"You fight as dirty as you talk."

"I fight to win. Best keep that in mind."

"Let's cut the gab and get outta here."

He sliced an opening with the knife, and one after the other they emerged to be confronted by a tepee twice the size of theirs. Smoke poured upward from the smoke hole, and light glowed orange against the buffalo hide cover.

Men were smoking, talking, playing a board game. Raider fit his forefinger to his lips. Pickett scowled. "As if I didn't know 'nough to keep still."

"Shut up," rasped Raider.

As silent as shadows they slipped past the pony string and out into the open. The moon emerged, bathing the area in brightness. Raider cursed and ran. He had not covered ten yards before Black Derby's knife slipped from his belt and rattled to the ground. Pickett, following him, snatched it up.

"Give it here," snapped Raider.

"Fuck you."

Both had stopped momentarily. Arguing over the knife would be insane, decided Raider, and he resumed running. Pickett followed close behind. For a man in his mid-forties, one accustomed to a steady diet of foul food and bad liquor, he showed surprising energy. Raider was soon puffing like a blown stallion.

Pickett swept by him easily. "Shake a leg, old boots," he sneered and cackled.

They ran more than a mile without stopping, without even slowing, until, his chest heaving, his lungs burning, screaming for air, Raider pulled up, dropped to his knees, and, supporting himself with his arms, hung his head and struggled to catch his breath.

Pickett stopped twenty feet ahead and, turning, came back to him. He leaned over. "What's the matter?"

"Don't . . . be . . . wiseass."

"Gulp in deep breaths."

"Shut up."

Raider got his wind back. Up on his feet, he cast a wary glance back at the camp. Nothing stirred. Black Derby must still be out cold, and Little Eagle or whoever had dispatched him to the tepee would probably be beginning to wonder what was delaying him.

Raider and Pickett ran at a leisurely gait side by side. The older man wasn't even breathing hard, Raider noted in annoyance. "We're goin' to DeLamar," he said.

"You are maybe, but not me. I got a warm bed waitin' on me in Silver City."

"I'll bet."

"Friends, whiskey, and a woman." He stopped short and whipped out the knife. "Got any objections?"

Raider held out his hand. "Give it here."

Pickett grinned demonically, raised the knife, catching moonlight on the blade, and brought it sharply down, narrowly missing Raider's hand.

"Bastard."

"You want it, take it. Just try." He half crouched, holding the blade point upward at an angle. He began to circle slowly. "Come on, Razorback, come take it. It's yours if you can. Try. Come on."

"You're a horse's ass."

"Horse's ass got the knife. Hee hee. Come on."

Raider turned his back and started to walk away. He could hear Pickett's feet move, hear him start after him. He could picture his face, the crazed leer, the knife coming up slowly, turning, pointing downward. One, two, three steps. Sucking his lungs full, Raider stopped abruptly, drove his right leg out to the side and moved sharp right. Stopped, pivoted on his left leg, and brought his right around, catching his attacker hard across both shins.

Down went Pickett, howling. Raider was on him like a cat, vising his wrist with both hands, squeezing, shaking the knife loose. It fell, and he snatched it up and tossed it away. Pickett recovered quickly and started up. Raider swung, catching him full in the temple, sending him sprawling and cursing.

"Sumabitch! Bastard!"

Up on his feet, head down, he came at Raider, driving both fists like pistons. Raider had height and reach on him, but that was all. Pickett was as agile as a ten-year-old, a barbed-wire bundle of muscle powered by an explosive temper, a fighting machine. Raider pulled to one side to avoid the flurry of knuckles coming at him, but in spite of his quickness still took three good shots to the head. He shook them off and came back, sledging him full in the jaw, stopping him in his tracks. Pickett's head jerked back, but his leer never left his face.

He never even felt it.

Back he came with a solid left flush in the gut. Raider whooshed and doubled over; it felt like a battering ram, driving through him and cracking his spine in two. Up came Pickett's knee, pounding him squarely in the face, upending him. Blood spurted from his nose; his mouth quickly filled with it. He spat out a tooth.

Pickett hovered over him, cackling. He raised one leg, then down it came. Raider twisted out of the way, swinging up on hands and knees, reaching, grabbing his leg, pulling, toppling him. Grabbing a handful of sand, Raider flung it in Pickett's face. Pickett sputtered, spit, cursed. Raider was up on his feet, driving one, two, three shots at his head, missing the first, glancing the second, the third snapping his head to one side.

The hole deserted by his tooth felt like a red-hot iron had been thrust into it. He spit out more blood. His face rang with pain, radiating back into his brain, dispersing, filling it. His head felt as if it would explode. Dizziness took hold. He swayed, battling it, fighting it off. But the sequence gave Pickett the few precious seconds he needed to recover and get back up on his feet swinging.

Toe to toe they stood battering each other. Never in his life, fighting all types, men hard as rock, solid sinew, gristle, flesh like plate steel, never never had he hit anything like this Ira Pickett, this leering, growling, taunting fighting machine. On he came relentlessly. Shot after shot seemingly hadn't the slightest effect. He was impervious to injury, insensible to pain.

He was, Raider concluded wearily, not human.

Raider smashed Pickett flush in the nose, powering his fist over a distance of nearly two feet, putting all the strength and hatred he could muster into it, squashing it, feeling the cartilage shatter under his knuckles. But Pickett didn't even blink. Blood spurted from his nostrils, draping his mouth. Out came his tongue, licking it from corner to corner, his leer widening.

"Hee hee hee hee hee."

Raider quickly became so exhausted his arms felt like steel rails. His face burned with pain. He choked on blood and spewed forth a mouthful. It struck the oncoming Pickett full in the face. For an instant he looked as if a liquid bandanna was laid over it, masking it. Then through it came his devilish smirk. Goaded to fury by the reaction, Raider swung a haymaker, putting every last ounce of his waning strength into it, bringing it around just above shoulder level, catching him on the side of the head, snapping it down onto his shoulder. Pain struck Raider's hand, his knuckles exploding with it. Pickett grinned on, and came back swinging, catching him in the shoulder, spinning him around, tangling his legs. Down went Raider on all fours. Up came Pickett's boot to lift his jaw up into his blood-smeared face. Raider jerked back just in time. Up rose the kick higher, higher. Out flew Raider's hands, catching his boot, lifting, lifting, upsetting him, dropping him on his rear. Still Raider held fast, still he lifted and lifted to the foot's full height, the leg now vertical. Spinning about, he twisted it, winding it, setting Pickett screaming, beating the ground with his hands. Twisting, twisting, till a loud, ominous cracking stopped him.

"Sumabitch! Bastard! Bastard, bastard, bastard!"

A shot. They froze. Three men came riding up. Raider took one look through painful eyes, swiped at his bloodied face with the back of his hand, spit blood, and sank into himself as he recognized the man in the forefront. His face, his leer, were unmistakably Pickett's. As if he needed confirmation, Pickett cheered in triumph.

CHAPTER TEN

Doc's common sense overcame his outrage toward Leroy
Blodgett for his obstinacy. Upon leaving Joshua Kincaide's
studio, he mounted his horse and headed back to DeLamar
at a gallop. Linking up with Raider would have to wait.
First he had to find Blodgett and the other operatives and
tell them what Kincaide had told him. For their own good
the townspeople's "uprising" had to be nipped in the bud.
He, Blodgett, and the others would have to confront them
and somehow persuade them that their taking the bull by
the horns would be unwise and for some of them fatal.
What arguments could they raise against the enterprise?
Offhand he couldn't think of one that sounded convincing.
The farther he rode the more it appeared it would take
some kind of action on the Pinkerton's part. Perhaps they
should take Abington into temporary protective custody.
Whatever was decided, Blodgett's stubborn refusal to interfere in Silver City's internal affairs would have to be
shelved. Bullheaded he might be, but he wasn't stupid, and
there was no way he could close his eyes to the bloody

outcome that would surely result if nothing was done to stop the townspeople. If he ignored the problem he would have to answer to Allan Pinkerton. Doc would see to that.

The look in Joshua Kincaide's eyes, his refusal to even consider jettisoning the plan or to discuss it further with him was most disturbing to Doc. He seemed blind to the threat of the outlaw horde. It was almost as if they didn't exist, that Abington and his deputies were the only ones they needed to worry about. He couldn't buy their attitude for a moment, but he could understand why they thought as they did. They were past anger. The dam of their frustration had collapsed. Talking to Joshua it was clear that he didn't care what happened to him just as long as they could pull Abington down and break his hold on their town once and for all. If the sheriff was killed, if others died in the effort, even innocent women and children, so be it. Wasn't sacrifice always the price of violent change?

"Not this time, Joshua."

Blodgett and the others were not in DeLamar. He checked with Marshal Watts. He hadn't seen them that morning, but one of his deputies had sighted them leaving town, heading toward Silver City. Doc hadn't met anyone riding back, but that was nearly four hours later. They may have started for Silver City, but he'd be willing to bet his pay they'd cut off the road partway there to begin circle-searching.

He started back toward Silver City, picking his way slowly down the dusty road, looking for multiple tracks turning off. He found them a mile from his destination, followed them, lost them, found them again. It was almost eight in the evening when he finally caught up with the group. Seven men, including the two slightly wounded in the Patchett ranch battle and Leroy.

Blodgett hailed Doc with a broad smile. "Change your mind?" he asked amiably.

Doc pulled up in front of him. The sun had been beating down on his bare head all afternoon. He had lost his derby in the fight, a slug drilling through the front and out the back of the crown as it lay on the ground a few feet from him, and he hadn't gotten around to replacing it. He felt a trifle ill, but was determined to ignore it, as resolutely as he would ignore the temptation to criticize Blodgett for his stand that morning. He related his conversation with Joshua Kincaide.

"Is he serious?"

"Worse, Leroy. He's rapidly working himself into a state verging on outright fanaticism, as if he were taking up the banner for a holy war, a crusade."

"You're exaggerating."

"You should have seen his eyes. Tonight when they storm the sheriff's office I'm sure he'll be in the forefront of the mob, a prime target."

"Did he say what time tonight?"

"Not exactly, although I'm sure they've scheduled a time for a meeting, and after they talk awhile and get everybody stirred up, they'll march on the office. When I tried to put the kibosh on the whole idea, he abruptly lost all interest in discussing it. I got the feeling that if he weren't a gentleman he would have thrown me out of the house."

"Do you think Abington'll get wind of it?"

"I'll bet he has already. How do you keep a thing like that secret?"

"You realize, of course, we really shouldn't meddle. Our instructions in this assignment couldn't be more explicit. The Southern Pacific doesn't care a fig about Abington or Silver City and its problems."

"Leroy. . ."

"All right, all right. I confess after you went storming off this morning I thought about the situation. It's practically all I've thought about all day."

"And concluded I was right?"

"I didn't say that."

"Then I was wrong. It's got to be one or the other."

Blodgett sighed in obvious impatience. "The longer you work with Raider the more like him you get—everything black or white, cut and dried."

"I'm lucky. Everybody in the agency should have a chance to work with him. Even you could improve your skills."

Blodgett sniffed. "You're entitled to your opinion."

"Can we save any discussion of him for another time? It'll be getting dark soon."

Blodgett screwed up his handsome face in thought.

Pondering their next move, mused Doc. He promptly relieved him of the need to concoct a strategy. "Let's head for Silver City. We'll take Abington and his deputies into protective custody. When we first met he mentioned he had four full-timers and two men who helped out when needed. We'll take him and whoever's with him."

"But where, Doc?"

"Anywhere, just out of there. Kincaide and his friends can stew and steam all they like. This way nobody will get hurt."

"We can't nursemaid Abington forever."

"We can hold him till we're able to talk some sense into the townspeople. Not Joshua, I mean the mayor and the judge. Hopefully, given the time, we can come up with some way of neutralizing Abington and satisfying everybody."

"He'll put up a fuss, we'll have to take him at gunpoint."

"Of course."

"We really have no authority."

"It's the only way, Leroy."

"I suppose. Only then what?"

"What do you mean?"

"We take him to another town, hide him, then what? Kincaide and the others will storm the office, they won't find him, what'll they do to us, do you think?"

"How will they know we were the ones who took him?"

"Don't be naive. In your conversation with young Kincaide you as good as implied you might if he refused to listen to reason. And he wouldn't. If Abington's gone he'll know who's responsible. And what about the outlaws the sheriff's protecting? Do you think they'll stand aside, let us blithely march in and grab him without lifting a finger?"

"Leroy, I haven't said there wouldn't be risk. Whatever happens, we're professionals, we should be able to handle it. Let's talk about it and decide the best way to work it. Only let's make it fast. It'll be dark soon. I'm sure that's all Joshua and his friends are waiting for."

Jason Pickett held his gun on Raider and ordered him to raise his hands. Raider tried,, but his arms refused to obey. His muscles all the way up to his shoulders were jelly. The boy fired at his feet. Raider glared and spat where the slug had hit.

"Leave him be, Jace," said Ira. "He's too weak. I beat him to a pulp, can'tcha see?"

To Raider's surprise Pickett had gotten to his feet and, standing somewhat unsteadily, tested his manhandled leg and found he was able to put his weight on it. He sneezed and smirked at Raider's awed reaction.

"Fooledja! It ain't busted after all. Take more of a man than you to bust one o' these bones. Asa, Willis, Jace, this here's a real live Pinkerton detective, been trackin' us all the way up from Battle Mountain. He's one o' them was in the express car when we busted in."

Raider recognized all three.

"He don't look like no detective to me," sneered Jace. He had dismounted. He approached Raider and inspected him. "You a Injun detective? Ha ha."

Again Raider ignored him. With the tip of his tongue he probed the hole deserted by his tooth. Jace took a step forward and, hauling off, slapped Raider so hard he knocked him sprawling. Jace laughed, and Asa joined in. Willis McColl only stared. Raider struggled up to hands and knees.

"You best answer the boy when he asts a question," cautioned Pickett.

"He can go to hell and take you three with him," Raider said through clenched teeth.

Jace started for him, but his father intervened. "Still fulla piss and vinegar, eh? Leave him be, young-un, we need him alive, need him to swap for two o' the boys his amigos captured out at the Patchett place."

"Who'd they get?" asked Asa Hudlin, his blank eyes peering out from under bushy red eyebrows. He wore batwing chaps and a greasy vest, and the stitching on his boots was so frayed it was barely able to hold them together. He carried a 10-gauge shotgun.

Bestride a roan mare alongside him, Willis McColl leaned on his pommel and stared down at Raider without commenting. He had yet to utter a sound since they arrived. He could have been deaf and dumb for all Raider knew. His broad face was badly scarred, suggesting he had run afoul of more than one opponent's knife. A deep gouge at one corner of his mouth pulled it down, adding to his ugliness. He was chewing tobacco, rolling it about his mouth, spitting weakly, trailing drool down his bristle-studded chin.

"Don't know which two," replied Pickett. "Sheriff Nat didn't know, only that there was two and they're in jail in DeLamar."

"Who cares," said Jace. "We don't need 'em now. Let 'em rot."

"That wouldn't be Christian, young-un. We should at least try and spring 'em."

"Can't Nat?" asked Asa. "He can if he cares to."

"He says for us to try first. He says he don't wanta stir nothin' up with the Pinks hangin' round and all. Give me your six-gun, Asa. Just for borry. Them savages took both my irons."

"They get the Battle Mountain money?" Jace asked.

"Hell no, I'm takin' good care o' that. What about the six thousand we took from the bank in DeLamar?"

"It's safe back at the shack."

"Good, we're gonna need it. Boys, we're headin' for Californy."

"Hiiiiii-yeahhhhhh!" Jace swept off his hat and batted

the side off his leg, loosing a cloud of dust.

Asa grinned, while Willis continued studying his fists on his pommel without so much as a glimmer of change in his expression.

Jace sobered. "How come we gotta deal for them boys? What the hell you pay Abington for if he don't do nothin'?"

"Never mind."

Pickett went on to explain the reason for Raider's disguise, their capture by the Shoshones, their escape. He painted himself as the hero, and Raider as little more than excess baggage.

"Your brother Caleb back at the shack?"

"With the DeLamar money," said Jace, "case anybody comes nosin' round. We was all of us there waitin' on you. When you didn't come and didn't come we got worried. We been lookin' for hours. It's just dumb luck we bumped into you."

"Dumb luck for the Pink there. I was gettin' ready to finish him off for fair. I got to the shack hours ago. I'da been there when you showed only he come round. I captured him slick. Asa, Willis, get aholt o' him and calf-tie him belly down over one o' your mounts. He's crafty as a savage, so tie him good. We'll bring him back to the shack."

"What for?" asked Jace.

Pickett flared. "Didn't I just finish explainin'?"

"Marshal won't take him in no swap."

"Just shut your face. I'll do the thinkin', the thinkin' *and* decidin'. He'll come in handy for a hostage for some-thin', he's a Pinkerton!"

"Pinkertons find out, they'll be down on us like gnats." Jace shook his head disapprovingly.

"I'll worry 'bout that. I know what I'm doin', allus do. Stop tryin' to poke holes in every word I say."

Raider was tied hand and foot over Hudlin's horse in front of his saddle.

Pickett checked his bindings, then leaned close to his

face. "Thought you busted my ankle, didn'tja? You couldn't, you're not man enough. Couldn't hurt me a lick, hard as you punched. I don't let pain hurt me. I firms my mind 'gainst it like a Mandan *o-kee-pa* torture rite brave with the pegs skewered under their flesh. The worstest agony: bullet, knife, even the Pawnee lance I took in the shoulder back when, I don't feel nothin', on account I firms my mind."

"You're a horse's ass."

"And you're this horse's ass' pris'ner, who's gonna die sufferin' pain like you wouldn't b'lieve. Jace, I'll ride double with you. Let's get outta here 'fore them savages show."

Raider studied the ground. So tightly had Asa tied his wrists the circulation was cut off. Already his hands were beginning to ache, his fingers swell. He raised no protest. If he complained Pickett would only laugh. To hell with it, he thought. To hell with the case, the Southern Pacific, the job, the agency. To hell with life. A man could take so much and no more. It wasn't the breaking point, it was more the fed-up point, like when you eat too much and it feels like gorge rising in you, climbing your throat, threatening to spill out your mouth. He'd been in worse fixes in his time, hurt worse, in more pain, closer to death, but he couldn't recall ever feeling such discouragement before. It had him by the throat. He could feel it, could taste it like metal in his mouth. When he spit it stayed.

It was all bullshit: the danger, the pain and suffering, the humiliation. It wasn't bad enough they battered his body, bled him, and busted his bones and his teeth, they had to punish his soul, whip his spirit. Why did he let them, all the Ira Picketts in his time? Why choose to battle them? For what? The money? It was shit. The thrill of it? More shit, horseshit, fresh, steaming, and stinking. Only an imbecile signed on for the thrill, the adventure. What in hell was so exciting about being grabbed by savages, being beaten to a pulp, embarrassed, slapped by some nose-picking ninny barely out of swaddling clothes? What was so alluring about pain and suffering, fighting people you didn't even know. For who? The Southern-Pacific? The Great Northern? The Atch-Topeka?

He was a fool, and so was Doc. Twelve years of it. Twelve years that, taken case by case, bullet by bullet, wound by wound, wouldn't add up to a hill of beans in the palm of his hand. Twelve years that might have been spent building a real life for himself, building for the future, a good and productive life. Not this. It was like standing in a barrel running in place, pumping your legs up and down and getting nowhere, while someone you didn't even know took potshots at you. Was *this* what he left home for? What Doc went to college and strained his brain for?

His head bobbed as the horse ambled along. He began to feel dizzy. The ground seemed to liquify. The night moved closer, touching him, taking him into her folds. The voices of his captors, their laughter, their cursing seemed to fade so that presently he could barely make out a word. He had lost a lot of blood and was still losing it. Now he was losing consciousness.

CHAPTER ELEVEN

Doc, Blodgett, and the six other operatives approached the sheriff's office from the rear, stopping their horses a good twenty yards from the back door. Doc and Blodgett dismounted.

"Tom, Fred, get around front and get his horse," said Blodgett. "If you find more than one, bring the other back too. Bring them all. Doc, you'll come in with me. I'll do the talking." He paused and glanced about. It was getting dark rapidly. "Looks like we're just in time."

"Let's do it, Leroy," said Doc impatiently. He drew his .38 from his shoulder holster and held it against his thigh and slightly behind him as they approached the three steps leading up the little landing to the back door.

Blodgett knocked and went in. Three of the four cells were empty. Two men occupied the fourth. They came running to the bars.

One recognized Doc. "The Pinkertons, thank God!"

"What happened?" asked Blodgett, peering through the

open inner door to the empty front office. Both men erupted excitedly.

"They came and took the sheriff!"

"The judge, Eb Hurtlemeyer, Kincaide the photographer, a whole flock."

"Locked us up, knocked him over the head, and hauled him out of here!"

"Which way'd they go?"

"Don't know, we couldn't see back here. But not west toward DeLamar."

"Probably north toward Murphy. They're crazy, like a swarm of hornets. They're going to string him up!"

"We seen the noose."

"They had torches, shotguns, rifles. There must have been forty or fifty."

"When?" burst Doc.

"Not ten minutes ago."

"Let's go, Leroy."

"Let us out!"

"You stay put, you can't get hurt in there."

Protests dinning in their ears, Doc and Leroy ran out. Seconds later they were galloping north. Silver City slipped farther and farther behind.

When Pickett, his friends, and his son reached the shack with their prisoner they found it in darkness.

"I thought you said you left Caleb to guard the money?" rasped Pickett.

"We did. Maybe he went into town."

"He's stupid if he did. Well, don't just sit there starin' your eyes out at me, get down, get in there and check."

They dismounted. Jace ran inside and lit a lamp. Pickett lifted Raider from Asa's horse like a sack of barley. He was only half conscious; he fought to stay awake, determined not to give Pickett the chance to ridicule him. His wrists and ankles remained tied. Pickett slung him over one shoulder, went inside, and dropped him heavily in a corner.

Jace was checking under the table in the middle of the floor. "It's still here."

"It better be. You don't walk out and leave that kinda money where any joker passin' by can march in and steal it. You oughta know better."

"It's Caleb's fault, he was s'posed to guard it."

"I'll settle his hash when he comes back. All right, Asa, Willis—"

It was as far as he got. Riders were coming through the narrow pass into the area. Pickett joined the others in the doorway. Raider could see through their legs in the moonlight. Four men had arrived.

At the sight of them Pickett spat and muttered. "Wouldn'cha know."

They dismounted and came forward. Raider guessed them to be the remnant of the gang, the ones who had successfully fled the Patchett ranch when Doc, Blodgett, and the others attacked. Only four? he wondered. Maybe the others, if there were any, had either died of their wounds or pulled out. It was obvious that even four were too many for Pickett's liking.

"Ira, where the hell you been?"

"Right here, Omar, in and out." He nodded to and addressed the others in turn.

"We was begining to think you cut out on us."

"That's a helluva thing to say, Omar Belding, that kinda talk riles me. You can't blame us for them Pinks comin' at you whilest we was over to DeLamar."

"Yeah, well neer mind 'bout that, we come for our money."

"What money?"

"What dya think? The Thunder Mountain job. You said there was near six hundred bucks. There's nine o' us left; that's near to seventy bucks apiece."

"It's closer to sixty. I'm leader, I get double. That was the 'greement. Whatcha want with a stinkin' sixty bucks for? Nickels and dimes. Not 'nough to keep you in liquor a week, Chrissakes."

"You won't get no argument from me on that, Ira. The job was a bust, but it's nobody's fault. We been thinkin', we hear you got six thousand in that little side job over to DeLamar."

"Who says?"

"It's all over town," said another man. The others nod-ded.

"You heard wrong. There wasn't more'n twelve hundred bucks in that cracker box."

"Six thousand," repeated Omar.

"You callin' me a liar?"

"Whatever there was, we want our share."

They had been talking just outside the door. They gradually drifted inside. Jace lit a second lamp.

Pickett stood staring at Omar. His expression said he couldn't believe his hearing. "*You* want a share in *our* job? You crazy, Omar? You been drinkin' or what? What right you got to a red cent from DeLamar?"

"Every right. We worked our asses off on that train. For what? Sixty lousy bucks a man? And woulda been a third o' that if we hadn'ta run into them Pinkertons. Fair's fair." He snaked out his Colt, pressing the muzzle against Pickett's belly. "Whatever you got, show it. Lay it on the table and we'll divvy it up. Right now, Ira."

He cocked. Pickett stared down at the gun and smirked. "You're crazy as a gopher, Omar Belding, must be if you think you're gonna get money outta me you're not 'titled to. Sides, it's not here. You think I'd be fool 'nough to stash it in this dump?"

"Where is it?"

"Where it's safe. Where you'll never find it."

"He's lyin', Omar," said one of the others. "Look at his eyes. Biggest liar on two feet, and he's lyin' now. It's here someplace."

"Start lookin'," said Omar tightly. "Jace, Asa, Willis, if you know what's good for you you won't try nothin'. You do and this old boy'll be dead 'fore he hits the floor, and you'uns'll catch the same."

Pickett laughed in his face, but was cut short. A scream went up outside, followed by a chorus of shrill cries. Fire arrows came arcing down, landing in the tall grass in front of the shack. One then another struck the iron roof, rolling off it harmlessly to the ground. The horses became frantic, walleyeing the fires, milling about nervously, whinnying. Untethered and unhobbled, they began to run. Led by Pickett's mare they stampeded toward the narrow opening. No sooner was the last one out of sight then a host of Indians carrying torches came running in, screaming their lungs out, led by Black Derby. In the glare of the torchlight Raider could see a huge black eye, incurred when Pickett had stomped him unconscious.

"Sumabitch!" burst Pickett. "They followed us, found where we parlayed, and tracked us to here!"

Omar Belding had lowered his gun. He turned and fired. A brave in the act of hurling his spear screamed and dropped. The spear whooshed through the open door, passing between Omar and Pickett, lodging in the rear wall, vibrating to rest. Out came every piece of hardware, directing a barrage at the onrushing savages. Down on one knee, Asa let loose with his 10-gauge, blasting a brave full in the chest, knocking him flat kicking, screaming, dying. At least thirty braves armed with bows and arrows, spears and rifles, had come rushing into the pocket. Others ringed the area up top, hurling down flaming torches and showering Omar and another man with arrows when they foolishly stepped out the door. In seconds both their corpses resembled pincushions.

"Pickett, untie me!" exclaimed Raider. "Pickett!"

"Fuck you! Can'tcha see we're busy?"

"Untie me, gimme a gun, let me help."

"Screw you!"

"Gimme a fightin' chance, for Chrissakes!"

"I give you a gun you'll backshoot me."

"I won't, word o' honor, untie me!"

Asa glanced at Pickett. To Raider, watching, it seemed he was mutely repeating the request.

Pickett barked at Jace, "Untie him."

"Pa . . ."

"Do like I say!"

Jace jerked out a knife. Raider consciously shrank from it, igniting a smirk on the younger man's face. He cut Raider's bonds. Raider quickly rubbed the circulation back into his ankles and wrists. Willis tossed him a Peacemaker and went to his rifle. Raider checked the chambers, bellied down, and pulled forward on his elbows. The action sent pain lancing to every corner of his body. He felt as if a boulder had rolled over him. Planting the pistol butt on the floor, he raised the muzzle slightly and shot an oncoming brave full in the chest. He stopped like he'd slammed into a wall, teetered briefly, dropped his Henry, and sank slowly to the ground. As he went down, who should pop up directly behind him but Black Derby. Not only was his eye blackened, but the cheek under it was badly swollen, broken by Pickett's boot heel.

One of the two surviving visiting outlaws edged toward the open door and raised his gun. And fired. Black Derby, now within ten feet of the door, was hit and briefly stopped, but his right arm, rising, clutching a tomahawk, continued moving upward. He let fly. It tumbled through the air with an eerie swishing sound and found its mark, lodging squarely in his attacker's face, splitting his skull like a melon. Down he went, driving the tomahawk deeper into his brain as it struck the floor.

The defenders were outnumbered four to one, but their vastly superior firepower was begininng to tell. The fire-blackened ground was strewn with dead Indians. The few survivors were retreating, backing into the narrow passage-way and out of sight. The Indians overhead gave up their firebombing. A score of fires, fanned by the breeze swishing down into the pocket, were rapidly merging, creating a wall of flame in front of the shack. Before Pickett could stop them, the infuriated, bloodthirsty Willis, Asa, and the fourth surviving visitor had bolted out the door, rushing through the flames to the opening.

"Asa! Willis! You goddamn fools! Come back here! Asa . . . Jace, go after 'em."

"Pa . . ."

"Do like I say! Git!" He kicked him out the door. "Fetch 'em back and pronto!"

He talked to Raider without turning. "Them savages is clever as hell. They only runned out to draw them damn fools with 'em, right? They did. They're waitin' out there to bushwhack 'em."

He turned slowly, smiling. His smile peeled from his face as his eyes found the black eye of Willis's gun in Raider's hand.

"You doublecrossin' bastard! You give your word o' honor."

"Not to back-shoot you. I got no intention to. Drop the gun."

"You . . ."

Raider fired, knocking the gun from his hand.

Pickett pulled his hand down sharply, cursing him. "You busted my hand!"

"Bullshit. How could that be? I'm not man 'nough to break your bones, remember? Go on outside."

"Like hell, they're still up top. They'll kill me."

"Do as I say or *I* will!"

"You're a son of a bitch, you know that?"

Raider gestured with the gun. Pickett walked out two, three steps, shrinking his head into the gap between his shoulders, cringing, slowly looking upward.

"They're gone," said Raider. "Back in here. Turn over the table, get the money, and give it here."

'I shoulda killed you when I had the chance."

"You shoulda. You're not gettin' another."

Raider stuffed the bills in his shirt. The gold was in a small leather drawstring pouch. He looped the strings around his belt, letting the pouch dangle. "Let's go."

"You're crazy. You'll never get past the rock face. Asa, Willis, and Jace'll nail you to it."

"You won't live to see it."

"Bastard!"

Outside, Raider cast a last look around. The fires were rapidly dying, the grass by now all but completely consumed. He marched Pickett ahead of him to the opening.

"Hold it," he ordered. He listened fully twenty seconds. No sound came from the other end. "Get goin'."

"I trusted you. You gimme your word o' honor. I shoulda knowed better'n to trust a fuckin' Pinkerton."

"Shut up. Let's get one thing straight before we go one step further. You listenin'? I intend to take you back to Elko for the pleasure o' seein' you hang, but we both know I don't have to. I can put your light out right here and now without takin' one more step. You try anythin', Ira, anythin' at all, I'll kill you. That's a promise. Man to man. My word o' honor."

CHAPTER TWELVE

By the time Doc, Blodgett, and the other operatives got to where the townspeople had taken Sheriff Nat Abington, the number of outraged and vengeance-minded citizens had increased tenfold. People preceded the Pinkertons and followed them, stern and bitter-looking men on horse and muleback, families in wagons. Torchlight cast an eerie glow over the gathering assembled around a lone and ancient cottonwood nearly a hundred feet tall, its lowest limb ideally positioned for and mutely inviting a rope. The air fairly crackled with hatred; the crowd was a cauldron filled with it, stirred and simmering. The worm had turned, and with a vengeance. Loathing glowed in every eye directed at the hapless Abington. He sat his horse, his wrists bound behind his back, his broad face bathed with nervous sweat. Off to one side at the inner edge of the gathering Joshua Kincaide was conferring with three other men.

Blodgett, Doc, and the others neared the rear of the crowd. Blodgett drew his gun and fired in the air. "Make way there," he ordered. "Coming through. Make way."

116

People stared. Not a soul moved until he repeated the demand. They backed away grumbling, glaring at him, opening a narrow path for them. Blodgett led Doc and one other man down the gauntlet. So fiercely did people stare that Doc half expected a shower of stones. There were muttered comments; the words "the Pinkertons" buzzed about. They reached the open center of the gathering but did not dismount.

Joshua Kincaide confronted Doc. "We know what you're going to say, Mr. Weatherbee. We're not interested."

"Turn round and get outta here," said the man beside him.

A third pushed forward. "This is our affair."

Kincaide nodded. "You're outsiders."

"And you're murderers," said Blodgett quietly but firmly. "That's what you're about to commit here. You can tell your loved ones and your consciences it's justice, vengeance, anything you please, but in your hearts you know what it is. What you are." He waved his arm theatrically and raised his voice. "Lynching is murder!"

The crowd hooted derisively.

"Get them outta here," growled a voice.

"Keep outta what ain't your bus'ness!"

"Turn round and get out."

Fire in reflection leaped from chrome as gun barrels showed. The inner ring of onlookers moved forward. Kincaide raised both hands to stay them.

"Tell 'em, Weatherbee," rasped Abington. "Listen to him, folks. He's no friend o' mine, he's on your side, but he's trying to set you straight. You can't do this terrible thing. God Almighty's looking down on you and judging each and every one of you. Murder's the worst sin there is. Tell 'em, Weatherbee. Stop 'em. They don't know what they're doing."

"Gag him," ordered Joshua.

"Josh . . ." began Doc.

Kincaide waved him away. Abington protested, squirming in his saddle, whipping his head back and forth, fighting the gag.

"I don't want to die! Please! Don't do it, don't!"

The gag was knotted tightly in place. He struggled to talk through it, but his words were incoherent.

Doc dismounted and confronted Kincaide. "This has gone far enough."

"You're wrong, it's just getting started," muttered Kincaide venomously.

He glanced at Abington, and when his eyes returned to Doc they were afire with bitterness. So deep-seated was his hatred, so consuming, his face was ghastly to look at. He murmured through clenched teeth, "If you know what's good for you, all of you, get out of here. We're doing what has to be done, and you can't stop us. If you try you'll force us to deal with you harshly. Very harshly."

Four men in the front of the crowd holding rifles moved forward as one at his nod and leveled their weapons at Doc and the others.

Kincaide took out his watch. "You have sixty seconds to get out of here."

"We're not going anyplace," said Blodgett.

Doc nodded firmly. "I'll give you one last piece of advice, Joshua. You go through with this and we'll have no recourse but to report you to Boise. You'll be punished to the full extent of the law. The law is very clear regarding lynching. Hang a man without a trial and you will hang with one. All of you. Every one of you here is as guilty as the man who slaps his horse out from under him."

"Stop the jawin' and get on with it."

"Get them the hell outta here!"

"String him up!"

"Hang him, hang him!"

The words were quickly taken up and became a chant. Fists rose, the indictment rang forth, scowls of hatred carved every face. Doc glanced at Abington. He was quivering with fear, the sweat bursting from his forehead, his eyes so huge they threatened to pop from their sockets. The man holding his horse began backing it under the limb. The sheriff raised his eyes to look at the noose over him. The sight of it sent him into a paroxysm of dread. He fought his gag, his bonds, his fear. Watching, Doc's heart went out to him. Whatever he'd done, however reprehensible his crimes, his sins and depradations against the people whom he had taken an oath to protect, as deserving as he was of punishment for violating that oath, his punishment must not be lynching. For when a man is lynched the law is lynched along with him. One is inseparable from the other. The law is flouted, it is weakened, the inflexible is rendered flexible and everyone whom it protects sees that protection placed in jeopardy. Arrest, trial, conviction, punishment, even death as punishment, all recognize and abide by the law. Not lynching. This was the dark side of humanity showing itself; fine, decent, normally law-abiding people resorting to a vengeance no court could countenance, no right-thinking individual could accept.

The noose passed over the lowest limb and, hanging straight down, was lowered so that it framed Abington's terror-filled face. The free end of the rope was made fast around the ring of a harpoon hay fork imbedded in the ground. An elderly white-haired man, whom Doc took to be Judge Aldergate, sitting astride a palomino, rode up beside Abington. The crowning touch, reflected Doc: judge become executioner. Joshua had described Aldergate as wishy-washy. Tonight he had found his spine; his face betrayed the murder in his heart.

The chanting persisted. The judge placed the noose around Abington's neck. A cheer went up, propelled by a loud burst of applause. A preacher rode up on the other side of the condemned man. Doc was within fifteen feet of them but still could not make out what he was reading from his Bible. Abington's eyes had taken on the glazed look of one who had passed beyond fear into the vale that separates it from acceptance of the inevitable. The man was in shock. His sweat must feel like a skin of ice, Doc thought, and the tension knotting his thundering heart must be filling him with the dread that any second now it would burst, filling him with the hope that it would, and put him out of his agony.

The torches tongued the darkness. The unmoving air was suddenly stifling. The stars watched. The crowd, still chanting, pressed forward in eager anticipation. Doc lowered his eyes from the grisly scene.

Someone fired a shot. It was immediately followed by an ear-splitting and sustained barrage. Lead sang over the heads of the onlookers. Doc instinctively ducked.

"Outlaws!" a woman screamed.

Pandemonium erupted. The crowd broke, people stampeding in all directions, into each other. The weak were knocked down, the strong running over them, tripping, falling, screaming, bellowing. Armed men in the crowd turned their weapons on the attacking horde. And a horde it was. Doc caught a glimpse of them galloping forward in a line that looked as if it stretched a quarter of a mile, galloping, yelling, firing. He flattened, his cheek pressed hard against the ground. Somebody stepped on his back; he imagined he could feel his spine cracking under the weight. He was kicked in the head. A man crouched directly in front of him busy loading his rifle was shot in the forehead. Down he went, a look of amazement on his face.

Doc craned his neck to look back at Abington still sitting his horse with the noose around his neck. Three crimson spots spattered his tan shirt. His eyes were closed, his expression peaceful. He was dead. He slumped slightly forward, only the rope about his neck preventing him from falling.

Judge Aldergate lay face down on the ground beside him, the lower half of his body concealed by the body of his palomino. The preacher had been hit with a shotgun shell; it had torn away the right side of his face, rendering it gore, stretching from his hairline to his neck.

The crowd was returning fire in earnest. The attacking line dispersed. Outlaws dropped from their saddles, horses

whinnying, milling about, and, when freed of the burden
of their riders, bolting away, wisely distancing themselves
from the arena of slaughter. Gunsmoke gathered in a gos-
samer blue cloud. The din was frightful, the carnage in-
credible.

Gun in hand, Leroy Blodgett crept up beside Doc.
"Great God in heaven!"

"I knew this would happen if it got this far, I just knew."

"Say your prayers, Doc, we'll never get out of here
ali—"

A stray shot stopped his mouth, freezing it open, the
slug plowing into his right temple, whirring through his
brain, and exiting his left temple. He had raised slightly on
one elbow as he spoke. Hit, his body stiffened. His mouth
slowly closed, letting his last breath escape. His eyes
stared questioningly at Doc, asking, Did it happen? Was I
shot? Am I to die? Must I? Doc?

CHAPTER THIRTEEN

Raider had walked his prisoner more than a thousand miles, or so it felt. It was actually just under twenty when the scattered lights of tiny DeLamar began pricking the darkness. Leaving the shack and the pocket, he had sent Pickett forward, half hoping that Asa, Willis, and Jace were waiting on the far side of the narrow pathway across the face of the rock and, prey to impulse, would shoot at the first one coming out. Why they should do such a thing made no sense, but so weary was he as he started out, so wracked with pain, that his brain was too exhausted to give him any thoughts that weren't muddled.

When they emerged from the cover of the rocks and started across the narrow way it was to discover that no one was waiting. Pickett called to his son and, ignoring Raider's threat to shoot him if he did it a second time, called again. But no one was around. None of the three, no Indians, no ponies, nothing but the stars and moon above, the desolate land below, and the brooding mountains.

They had set out for DeLamar talking, arguing, berating

each other, flinging insults and sarcasm, any words that came to mind to help keep them awake and upright. So exhausted was Raider, halfway to their destination, he began to toy with the idea of shooting Pickett, killing him then and there before he himself collapsed. Were he to pass out, Pickett would be on him in an instant, wrenching the gun from him and emptying it into his head.

How did he do it? Raider asked himself. How did he walk with that spring in his step, with the energy normal people had only after a good night's sleep and a hot breakfast? If he was hurting at all he didn't show it—he didn't limp, didn't favor any part of him. He held his head erect, his eyes were clear, he was alert, his smile remained firmly fixed.

DeLamar's lights twinkled invitingly.

"You'll never make it, Razorback. You're comin' to the end o' your rope fast. Look at you, you can hardly stand, let alone walk."

He was right, reflected Raider ruefully. He felt dizzy; he was beginning to stagger. The ground appeared to heave like the deck of a storm-tossed ship, lifting one side, then the other, forcing him to walk the gully formed between, picking his way, struggling to maintain his balance. His legs felt like water all the way up to his hips. He sweat furiously; he was sick to his stomach. He pictured blood sloshing against the walls. His tooth hole ached, as did his upper body; his rib cage felt as if it had been pushed through a clothes wringer. The gun in his hand weighed fifty pounds, then sixty. He had to grip it with both hands to keep the barrel level and aimed at Pickett's back six paces ahead of him. He finally ordered him ten paces ahead, then quietly holstered the gun. He stumbled and fell to one knee, drawing as he dropped. Pickett spun around, leering.

Up came the gun. "Try it, Mr. Stink. Please."

"Bastard!"

"Turn around and keep goin'."

"End o' your rope. You've lost a lot o' blood. A whole bucketful. Feel weak as a kitten, don'tcha?' You should see yourself. Behind all that blood clotted round your mouth you're white like a sheet. You don't see me white like no sheet. I look healthy, like I was this mornin'. That's 'cause I firms my mind 'gainst pain."

"Shut up, you asshole."

"Firms it, keep it from me. I can't be hurt by what I can't feel."

"I said shut up. So help me I'll kill ya!"

"I feel fitter'n a fiddle, I do."

Raider fired. The bullet slammed into the ground between Pickett's feet.

He jumped and cursed. "I turn the tables on you, I'll kill you screamin'."

They were approaching Marshal Watt's office from the rear. Raider scanned the sky. The North Star ascending, circling the Big Dipper counter-clockwise, had reached the position of the number 2 on the face of a clock. And that, he knew, was the time: 2 A.M. The marshal would be home in bed, the office probably locked up tight for the night. When they reached the back door Raider stopped Pickett and thought a moment, then started him down the alley flanking the office on the right. His heart rose; light showed in the side window. He marched him around front. A young deputy, badge in place, his Adam's apple riding his throat, pimples strewn about his face, his skin like a girl's, too young to have ever felt a razor, greeted them with a mystified look.

"Who?"

Raider pushed Pickett inside. "Where's the marshal?"

"Home in bed. It's past two in the morning."

Raider dug the six thousand out of his shirt, stacking it on the desk.

"You an Indian?"

"What the hell do *you* think? I'm a Pinkerton. This is the money stolen from the bank. This is the piece o' dirt that did the holdup. Him, his two sons, and two others.

Lock him up, count the money, and give me a receipt."

"Don't listen to him!" exclaimed Pickett. "He's no Pinkerton—I am. He stole my I.D. He's got it on him. My name's Raider. He's nothin' but white scum posin' as a Injun. He's wanted for rapin' and killin'—"

Raider swung and smashed him in the face. "One more word outta you and I'll beat you to death."

"Big man. Bastard!"

"You gonna lock him up or you gonna stand there with your face hangin' out til sunup?"

He didn't wait for his answer. He marched over to the key ring hanging on the wall beside the inner door. He tossed it jangling to him. "Do it!"

Pickett was locked up in the cell next to his two men. They were asleep when the deputy opened his cell door. The sound of it closing and locking woke them. They sat up yawning, rubbing their eyes, and then gawking with amazement at sight of Pickett. He turned from them and sat down on his cot.

"Ira . . ."

"Shut up."

"What the hell you doin' here?"

Both were up on their feet, seizing the bars separating the cells, gaping at him.

"Go back to sleep, you two," growled Raider. "You can jaw with him in the mornin'." He yawned. "Pickett, I'm puttin' you on ice here till tomorrow noon. I need my beauty sleep. I'll be back then to collect you. You and me and your two friends here'll be headin' for Elko. Who knows? Maybe by the time we get there they'll see the light and agree to testify 'gainst you."

"Bullshit. As for you, you're gonna be headin' for hell in a handbasket when I turn the damn tables on ya, just see if I don't."

"I'll be holdin' my breath. Sweet dreams, all o' you, and sleep tight." He grabbed the deputy's elbow and steered him out front, closing the door behind them. "What time does your boss come in in the mornin'?"

"Around eight."

"You're on duty till then, right?"

"Yup. I wouldn't be. We don't generally do duty twenty-four hours, but the marshal says we got to until those two inside are released to the custody of the Pinkertons. You say you're one?"

Raider showed his I.D.

"How come you're dressed like an Indian?"

"It's a long story and not very interestin'. I gotta go. Gotta lie down before I fall down. I got a room at the Bluebird House with a bed that's gonna feel better than a pretty girl's arms. Good night." He started out the door, stopped, and turned. "I sleep, you stay awake. He's trickier'n a fox. Don't talk to him, don't open that door for nothin'. If he gets out, if any of 'em do, you'll answer for it. And you'll never pin another badge on as long as you live."

The deputy gulped, agitating his Adam's apple, and nodded. "I swear, I won't even open the door. Good night."

Doc opened his eyes. The room revolved slowly, the stained and in some places loosened flowered wallpaper blurring, the blossoms merging. He closed his eyes. His left side throbbed just under his heart. Fear shot through him: he could not feel it beating. His right leg ached just above the knee on the outside. With his eyes closed, his hearing became more acute. He could hear voices outside the closed door, feet shuffling, chairs moving, a pan or something else metallic dropping. He heard the outer door open. Again he opened his eyes. A man was bending over him. He wore pinch glasses, the black ribbon trailing down, coming to rest on Doc's chest. Worry etched his mottled features. His lips were plum-colored and his upper teeth bit lightly into the lower one as he nodded to himself, as if to confirm a decision reached.

Doc tried to speak, but his mouth was stuffed with cotton, or so it felt. It was extremely dry, and when he investigated it with his tongue his taste buds actuated bitterness. The smell of ammonia thrust its way up his nostrils into recognition.

"Don't dry to dalk," said the doctor. "I vill answer your kveshtions so you von't haff to ask dem. You are in Murphy. Der vas a shootoud a vew miles soud uff town. Vot am I zaying, a vull-scale battle, a vor!"

At least a hundred dead and double that number wounded, including women and children. Leroy Blodgett dead and all the others. He alone among the eight a survivor. For how long? his eyes asked worriedly. Two wounds, the one under his heart the worst, driving through his rib cage and lodging just under the heart in a spot well out of reach of a probe, too deep and in too critical an area to go after right away. The slug in his leg routine, already removed. Considerable loss of blood. Better off than most of the other wounded, however, and he would live. But he'd be flat on his back for at least three weeks.

Dr. Von Zell had bits and pieces of Silver City's night of horror. The outlaws had attacked in the hope of rescuing Abington. In the wild shooting that ensued, he, the judge, the minister, Joshua Kincaide, and dozens, scores of others, including Blodgett and the other six operatives, were slain. At least fifty of the attackers had been gunned down by the townspeople. Von Zell had not seen the battleground, but those who had described it variously as Bull Run, Aceldama, the floor of a vast open-air slaughterhouse, and worse. As the doctor talked on, Doc began to lose consciousness. Someone knocked and the door opened, taking Von Zell's attention. He muttered and went out. Doc slept.

Raider awoke and slowly, gingerly, tensing against the expected sudden resumption of pain, sat up. Pain came, but with far less intensity than the night before, more of a dull throbbing than the sharp stabbing and flashing that had previously assaulted him all over his body. He washed and brushed his teeth and felt fair, the nausea gone from his stomach, his head clear, with no threat of dizziness. The bones had come back to his legs.

He rolled up his Indian garb and dropped it out the window into the trash-littered alley below. He dressed, went downstairs, and checked out. He ate a sumptuous breakfast—six eggs, a rasher of bacon, half a loaf of toast, six cups of coffee.

It was twenty-five past twelve by the clock in the jewelry store window across the street from the diner when he emerged and set out for the marshal's office.

He found Watts sitting at his desk, his feet up, reading a pink *Police Gazette*. Raider introduced himself and showed his I.D. The marshal's congenial expression faded perceptibly. He licked his lips and straightened in his chair.

"We, ah, had a little accident shortly after you left here last night."

Raider stiffened. "Pickett got away."

"No, no, he's still in custody. Nobody got away. Ahh . . ."

"Spit it out."

"Vernon was out front here, the way he tells it. The inside door was closed. He claims he didn't hear a blessed thing. He could have dozed off. It *was* late. Around three, maybe a little after, he checked inside. The two your partner Weatherbee and that fellow with the curly blond hair brought in from the shoot-out at the Patchett ranch, they were on the floor."

"What in hell are you talkin' about!"

"Just what I goddamn said. You deaf?"

"How. . ." Raider stopped and started for the door, grabbing the knob, whipping it open.

"They're not there now. When I came in this morning Vernon and I got some help and hauled them off to Oberdecker's Funeral Parlor. Don't look at me like that, they were dead all right, it wasn't any trick. Strangled."

"Pickett!"

"He says no, but it couldn't be anybody else. Could it?"

"Jesus Christ!"

"I'm sorry. We're responsible, of course. Vernon never dreamed he'd do something like that."

"It's my fault as much as his. I never shoulda let him lock Pickett up within reach o' them. He musta figgered they'd double-cross him. Once we got back down to Elko, they'd testify 'gainst him, help get the rope round his neck to save their own."

"You want to talk to him?"

Raider had closed the door. "Hell no, he'd only give me a song and dance. And the way I feel this minute if I get close 'nough to him to talk I'd likely strangle the son of a bitch. Man's the biggest bastard I've ever run into. Of all the rotten, livin', breathin' things crawlin' this earth, he's gotta be the second worst, right after a friggin' corpse worm, and not far after."

"He's sure been singing your praises since he woke up this morning."

"I only hope one thing. That I can get him down to Elko and rid of him without killin' him. It's not gonna be easy. In fact it'll be just about the hardest thing I've ever done." He sat down hard and shook his head. "Both dead! What a son of a bitch he is!"

"Did you hear about the battle royal?"

"What?"

"Out on the Murphy road last night. A bunch of law-abiding citizens in Silver City got themselves up a necktie party. Captured the sheriff and took him out to hang him."

"No!"

Watts nodded. "It's the gospel truth. People can stand so much and no more, and when they boil over all hell breaks loose. Did last night, I mean *all* hell. They got within an eyelash of hanging him, even had the noose around his neck, when that filthy rabble in cahoots with him that he protects—must have been a hundred of them—showed up and tried to stop it. A couple hundred people killed."

"The Pinkertons weren't there."

"They were. All of them. They rode out about ten minutes ahead of the outlaws and tried to stop the hanging. Word is they got stuck in between, caught in a crossfire. They say they were among the first ones killed."

"All?"

"Every one."

Raider died gradually, an inch at a time. Doc's smiling face rose up before him, his curly brim derby tilted at a rakish angle, a flower in his buttonhole, a pretty lady on his arm. She too was smiling. Light flashed, the powder exploded. The photographer squeezed his bulb, the picture froze and started to pull away, shrinking, the borders appearing. The breeze caught it, twisting it every which way, shrinking, shrinking, vanishing. . . .

"Doc!"

"Weatherbee. I remember him. Good-looking chap."

"You say he was killed?"

"All of them were, that's what I heard."

"Who says?"

"Calvin Parnell told me. You've met Calvin."

"He was there? How in hell does he know?"

"He heard—"

"You heard, he heard, everybody heard. Who the hell was there and saw? Who?" He jumped to his feet. "You don't know a goddamn thing, only what you 'heard.' He's not dead, he can't be. There had to be wounded. Where'd they take 'em? I'm talkin' to you, goddamn it, don't sit there like a bump on a log, answer me! Where'd they take the wounded?"

"Murphy would be closest."

Raider started out the door.

"Aren't you going," began the marshal just before it slammed, "to take your prisoner?" He continued after it did. "I guess not, I guess later."

Raider bought a little gray grulla and a Texas saddle for six dollars that looked as if a herd of longhorns had stampeded over it. He strapped it on and flew away to Murphy.

Dr. Von Zell was too busy to talk. "Can't you zee vot's

goink on all around you? I'm ub to my ears!"

"Weatherbee! Weatherbee!"

"Who?"

The doctor waved him away. They were standing in the center of the waiting room. It was mobbed with walking wounded, arms in slings, bandaged heads and shoulders and legs, crutches, canes. It looked like an army field hospital. Von Zell had turned his back on him to talk to a woman wearing a nurse's cap and cape. Raider grabbed him from behind around the waist and pulled him back.

"You're not goin' anyplace till you listen!" He hurriedly described Doc. Von Zell's glare softened into a perplexed expression. He lifted his glasses from his nose and began patting his lips with the edge of one lens. Perplexity gradually gave way to recognition.

"Oh, ja, ja, Vetterbee. In the coostum-made zoot, uff gourse. He's inzide, but you can't zee him now, he's azleep."

Raider brushed by him and burst inside.

He was.

"Doc, Doc, it's me!"

Von Zell followed him in. "Vot did I just zay!"

"Get the hell outta here. Leave us alone. Doc, Doc!"

Doc stirred, licked his lips, made a distasteful face and slowly awakened. "Rade . . ."

"Oh shid!" Von Zell threw up his hands and went out.

"You okay?" Raider asked. "You look terrible, like you're at death's door. What happened?"

Doc mumbled explanation haltingly, his voice barely above a whisper.

"And Leroy's dead? And the other guys?"

"Mmmm. And I'm flat on my back for the next three weeks until I'm strong enough to take the bullet out of me. It's about two whiskers below my heart."

"So let him take it out, what are you waitin' for?"

"It's too dangerous. I've lost a lot of blood."

"So've I, but you don't see me walkin' round with slugs in me. Leavin' it in is what's dangerous. Doesn't he know that? What is he, a friggin' horse doctor?"

"He's a good man, he knows what he's doing. I have to go along with what he tells me."

'It's bullshit, leavin' it in. Leave it in it'll poison your blood and finish you off. Shit, this screws up everythin'. I'm leavin' this afternoon to take Mr. Stink back to Elko."

"What about the two others?"

"We lost 'em. He reached through the bars and strangled 'em."

"He what?"

"Now all's left is him, and the quicker I get him back the better. Soon as I make sure Leroy and the other boys get themselves a halfway decent burial I'm on my way. After I deliver Mr. Stink I'll come back for you."

"What happened to Hudlin and McColl? What about his two sons?"

"We all had a small run-in with Mr. Feathers last night up in the hills. In all the to-do they flew the coop. I don't care, I got me the kingpin. He's what I wanted from the first; the hell with the small potatoes."

"You plan to take him back alone? You don't think they'll try to stop you? Maybe Hudlin and McColl can't be bothered, but his sons won't stand idly by and let you haul him off. I don't like it, Rade, it's risky as the devil. You've got a two-day trek ahead of you across some of the most barren country in the West. They'll be watching you, waiting their chance to pounce."

"Let 'em try. I'd love nothin' better than to blow them away right in front o' him standin' helpless watchin'. I've never wanted to take anybody in, see 'em strung up and dancin' the last waltz more than him, Doc. He gets to me, grinds me, he eats my gut with that sickenin' leer o' his. He's a mad dog. I can't worry 'bout his kids. If the one I haven't met isn't any savvier or gutsier than the one I have I got no problems with either."

"I don't like it, Rade."

"I know, you just said."

Dr. Von Zell came in. He eyed Raider fiercely.

"Enough! Ged oud und let him rest. He's shtill very veak."

"I'm goin'. I won't see you again before I leave, Doc, but I'll be back real soon."

"Oud!"

"I'm goin', I'm goin'. Hey, how come you don't take that slug out from under his heart?"

"Vot?"

"Rade . . ."

"I said—"

"I heard vot you zed. Vot are you, a doctor? You don't look like a doctor to me, you look like a trail bum. Now ged oud before I haff you trown oud!"

Raider returned to DeLamar to find that Marshal Watts had changed his thinking in regard to his responsibility in Pickett's capture. His subdued and somewhat condescending manner of earlier in the day had vanished.

"I really think I should detain him here on the bank robbery charge."

He followed this with a list of reasons for so doing. Raider only half listened. It was clear that with Abington no longer a threat to his authority, the marshal was suddenly becoming cocky. He was not just wearing his badge now but displaying it with a sense of professional pride.

Raider refused to be impressed. "Forget it. He belongs to the Southern Pacific."

"The man committed grand larceny in my jurisdiction."

"And I got you your money back, every cent. And brought him in. You didn't even go out after him. I made it clear to your deputy with the pimples last night I was stickin' him in here temporary. I'da made it clear to you only you were home poundin' your ear."

"I can get a court order."

"Get a whole basketful, I don't care. Him and me'll be outta here by the time you do. Show a little gratitude, for Chrissakes. I've put a big fat feather in your cap, and Abington's gettin' shot has put you back in the driver's seat with the whip in your hand. You can be marshal with pride now, no more shame. You can hold up your head, for Chrissakes. Who they gonna get to take Abington's place?"

"They're sending in a federal marshal. He'll be in charge until a new sheriff's voted in. Understand something, Mr. Raider. I'm not trying to hang on to Pickett just for my own purposes, just to deprive you of him. I'm trying to do you a favor, give you a chance to wash your hands of the man."

"How's about lettin' me decide if I wanta wash my hands?"

"Have you considered that his men and his two sons are still at large? They'll track you all the way to Elko, and before you get him there they'll jump you, probably kill you if that's what it takes to free him."

Raider laughed.

"What's funny?"

"Nothin', just that all of a sudden everybody seems to be worryin' about me travelin' with him. If his kids do show up, if the shootin' starts, he'll be the first to die. He knows that. He'll do everythin' he can to keep it from happenin', beginnin' with sendin' those two packin'."

The marshal chuckled.

"What's funny?"

"For a practical man, you sure know how to twist logic."

The door opened. In came Vernon. He greeted the marshal and flashed Raider a self-conscious smile.

"Pickett's leaving, Vernon. Mr. Raider is taking him back to Nevada."

"I know," he said. "Good luck, Mr. Raider. Only, if you don't mind my saying so, you'd best watch your hindside every step o' the way. His friends and his two sons are still on the loose."

"Oh for Chrissakes!" snorted Raider. He got up, waved and went out.

CHAPTER FOURTEEN

Raider had already informed Chicago of the deaths of the seven operatives. In line with agency policy, the bodies would be embalmed and held for seventy-two hours. Relatives would be informed by telegram from Allan Pinkerton, and if no request for shipment home was forthcoming, the deceased would be buried in the area where he had met his death. The chief would then send his personal message of condolence to the operative's wife or mother.

The sight of Leroy Blodgett's corpse lying in the funeral parlor in Silver City was particularly disturbing to Raider. Adonis looked handsome even in death. Raider had disliked him intensely in life, but seeing him brutally murdered softened his heart. He deserved better, much better than death too early in this out-of-the-way place, far from his loved ones. Doc had admitted that Blodgett had not wanted to involve them in Silver City's dilemma and had only reluctantly gone along with his, Doc's, thinking. His gun was still in his hand when they found his body. He had fired only one shot, the shot in the air to capture the crowd's attention when the group first got there. At thirty-one he was the oldest of the operatives who had come to assist Raider and Doc in the case.

Raider was particularly troubled by the fact that he had parted company with Blodgett in anger at the man. And he had died before either of them could apologize. It was unfinished business now unfinishable, a tooth that would always gnaw his conscience.

He could never remember hearing Blodgett's name without feeling his ire rise. Still, he wasn't a bad man, they simply rubbed each other the wrong way. Which was about as mildly as he could describe it. Neither had given the other a chance; their dislike of one another had become a bad habit, and reconciliation had never stood a chance. A pain in the neck, but a good operative, Raider conceded, pigheaded, perhaps, but with spleen, and a credit to the "eye that never sleeps."

Doc, too, thought about Leroy Blodgett, more or less sharing Raider's view of the man, though he had never had his partner's problem with him. He had had to talk Leroy into seizing the initiative, his conscience reminded him; had he not done so he and the others would still be alive. Lying in bed hour after hour Doc had nothing to do but think, reflect on the events of the night before, and speculate on what might have been. Regret simmered in him, and it was a relief when a knock sounded at his door.

Dr. Von Zell poked his head in and announced that he had a visitor. "A lady. You veel up to a visit?"

"Yes, who . . ."

He opened the door wider to reveal Alvina Kincaide. Doc's heart tugged in his chest. She looked like death, as if she'd been crying for hours. She tried and failed dismally to smile a greeting and came in. Von Zell left them in privacy.

"I'm so sorry," he began.

"I knew I shouldn't have gone to Gooding. Shouldn't have left him."

"How could you possibly know what he was up..." He stopped. "He didn't tell you."

"Not a hint. He didn't have to, I knew how he felt. I should have expected it. These last few weeks he was like a...a volcano, threatening to...you know. He despised Abington, but himself even more for letting it go on."

"As if he were solely responsible."

"He reached a point where he felt he was. It's silly, of course. I'm sure half the people in town felt the same way. You didn't really know him, I'm afraid. On the outside he was friendly, gracious, a perfect gentleman, basically as peaceable as anyone I've ever known. Even in anger, and he had a temper, I'd never seen him lift his hand against anyone. A pacifist, on the outside. Inside he was..."

"A volcano."

"He hardly ever talked about it to me. Oh, he'd start to, then catch himself. He knew how upset it made me, but it gnawed at him so. There were times he'd walk the floor at night. He'd go out and walk for miles by himself. To work it out of his system, I guess. It never did, nothing could."

"Why did you stay in Silver City?"

"I didn't want to, but wild horses couldn't make him leave. That would have been a mortal blow to his pride, his manhood, the last straw, complete surrender to Abington and the system, that's what Joshua called it. He saw leaving as the coward's way. I could never understand. The situation bothered him dreadfully, frustrated him, but he did nothing. What could he do? Still, he felt he had to stay. If the chance came to topple Abington he wanted to be here to use it. He couldn't run away with his tail between his legs. He said as much; he said he'd never be able to look me in the eye again if he did. He finally got his chance, God help us. Why? why?"

"He was a man, Alvina, in the fullest sense of the word. There are some things no real man can live with."

"He was a fool!"

"A martyr, perhaps. He chose his fate. He felt he had to

do it and went ahead. I tried to talk him out of it. We went out there to quash it, but it was useless. We might as well have talked to the wind."

"A pity you people had to get involved."

"There was no way to avoid it. But I have to disagree with you: he was no fool. He was a man, a very good man who had had his fill and couldn't take any more. I know it sounds lofty and philosophical, and perhaps even poppy-cock to you, but that's how I see it. Honestly."

"We should have left Silver City ages ago. We never should have come."

They talked on. He tried his best to reassure as well as console her, to paint Joshua as courageous rather than hot-headed, proud and principled rather than misguided. From her facial reactions it was all but impossible to evaluate his success. He wondered why she had come to him of all people. Surely she had friends in town whom she was closer to, in whom she could more readily confide. Why come to a stranger, for that was what he was, having only exchanged a few words with her in their one meeting? Perhaps she was going around talking to anyone who would listen, hoping it would help ease her shock and perhaps answer questions she was unable to find answers for herself. Leaving her husband and going to visit her sister was clearly on her conscience. He pointed out that she could scarcely blame what had happened on her absence. She was Joshua's wife, not his nursemaid. Many wives and husbands go away alone for one reason or another once in a while.

"I'm glad to see you're going to be all right," she said, abruptly changing the subject. "The doctor says you will be. And I am grateful. At least you tried to stop him." She smiled thinly. "Had I been there I would have told you you'd be wasting your breath." She sighed. "One thing troubles me more than anything else. I could see it coming. I really could."

"I'm sure you could. Anyone who knew him could."

"If it wasn't last night it would have been next week or

next month. But soon. He was getting near the breaking point."

She began to cry. She excused herself, got out a soggy hanky, and daubed at her eyes. Women crying invariably filled him with a sense of helplessness. He tried to console her, but it was useless. She became embarrassed. He sensed she thought she was making a spectacle of herself.

She finally left. His heart went out to her, and for a time after the door closed he berated himself for his failure to dissuade Joshua. When this turn of mind finally ran its course and he was able to reclaim his objectivity he found himself wondering why one invariably blames oneself for that over which one has no control.

And now with the nightmare behind him yet another worry impinged itself on his mind: Raider's taking Pickett down to Elko.

It wasn't until the middle of the afternoon that Raider was ready to leave DeLamar. He got hold of a horse for his prisoner and bought thirty feet of 3/8-inch Manila rope. Raider had planned that along his intended route they would not pass through any towns. They would sleep in the open, and at night he would tie Pickett and hobble their horses. They could bypass the Tuscarora Mountains to the north, but immediately beyond rose the Independence Mountains, and these they would have to cross just south of Monument Peak. It was either that or add another fifty to seventy-five miles to the journey.

The worst inconvenience he foresaw, the sole source of suffering, promised to be Pickett's mouth. If it got too bad he could always gag him, but he probably wouldn't. Their arguing would help pass the time, and Mr. Stink may have been rotten to the core, but nobody could accuse him of being a bore. He *was* colorful.

One good thing about the journey: until they reached the mountains Raider would enjoy a clear view of the land surrounding them for a considerable distance in every direction. If he slept with one eye open—and this he could

do for two nights running before exhaustion overtook him
—Pickett's sons would have a hard time sneaking up on
them. He could cover between forty and fifty miles before
darkness, about a quarter of the distance. The next day he
could probably come close to doubling that, but reaching
the mountains would slow them, and by then the horses
would be weary and impossible to push. Still, chances
looked very good that he'd reach Elko or come very close
to it before sundown the third day.

With more than half of today shot, he flirted with the
idea of delaying his start until the next morning, but he
finally decided that the sooner they started, the sooner
they'd get there. And the sooner Pickett would be off his
hands. The chief would be satisfied. Not overjoyed, not
even pleased. The assignment had cost them the lives of a
dozen good men, with only the one outlaw collected, but
he was the ringleader, and Raider would be bringing back
all but twenty-two dollars of the stolen money. Twelve
lives for approximately $600. Life could be distressingly
cheap in this line of work.

He had eaten lunch. Pickett had been fed in his cell, and
Raider packed dry food and coffee for the trip. He went to
the marshal's office to pick up his prisoner, and Watts
asked him to sign a paper acknowledging that Pickett was
being taken "out of the marshal's jurisdiction by the Pinkertons." Raider signed it, and the marshal unlocked Pickett's cell door and summoned him out.

"This place has never smelled so in the thirteen years
I've been marshal," whispered Watts to Raider out of the
corner of his mouth. "We're going to have to scrub down
the whole area here with carbolic soap and ammonia. On
your feet, Ira."

Pickett sat on the edge of his cot, eyeing one then the
other. "What if I refuses to go?"

"I'll whack you over the head and sling you over your
horse," said Raider. "You can ride belly down or rump, but
you'll ride, and I'll repeat the warnin' I gave you the other

night. You'll ride a few paces ahead o' me, and if you try
anythin' funny I'll shoot you."

"Sure."

"And if those nosepickin' kids o' yours show up I'll
blow your head off before they get within a hundred
yards."

"You better worry 'bout Asa and Willis McColl, too."

"I don't think so. I don't think they care two beans what
happens to you."

"They're the most loyalest o' my men, and the closest
to me. They'd ride through fire for me."

"Of course. Who wouldn't?"

The marshal's expression had become thoughtful. "I
could be making a big mistake, releasing him in your custody like this. I'm not talking about the bank robbery, I
mean the murders, him strangling those two."

"I didn't strangle nobody!"

"You really care about them?" Raider asked.

"You don't see no blood on these hands!"

"You gonna mourn 'em? Is DeLamar? You want this
stink to take root permanent?"

"Get him out of here."

"Let's go, Ira."

"Good luck," said the marshal at the back door. "And
keep a sharp eye on him."

"You tell him, Marshal. Y'hear, Razorback? You
gimme a inch and I'll take a mile."

"Shut up."

As he said it he sighed inside. He'd say it a hundred
times more over the next fifty hours.

Outside, Pickett took one look at the Mexican horse
Raider had bought for him and the Texas saddle and started
in. "Jesus, will ya look at that fleabag! Whata sight! Whata
bag o' bones. How'm I s'posed to ride that ridge back? It's
sharp as a plow blade. Look at them haunches, them
droopy ears. She must be fifteen years old if she's a day.
And look at that seat. Whyn'cha tie a flat rock on her back

for Chrissakes, be more comfor'ble than that piece o' junk. Visalia stirrups. Nobody uses them no more, don'cha know? They're the worst feet cripplers there is. Man, you are heartless, you pass off this billy goat and junk rig on me just to rile me, just to make the trip as uncomfor'ble as can be. Sheer torture!" His eyes drifted to Raider's horse. "That nag you got ain't much better, but a little. Tell you what we'll do here. I'll ride her, you ride this one. Hey, what's with the bandanna?"

"I'm gonna gag you."

"Like hell."

"If you don't shut up I will, I swear I will!"

"All right, all right, big man. Well, what's it gonna be? We gonna stan' roun' jawin' all day or are we leavin'?"

They made a little over forty miles before darkness. Raider found a campsite to his liking in a dry wash, where he could build a small fire without the flames being seen nearly three quarters of a circle around them. He tied Pickett's ankles so he could make coffee without having to eye him every second. The outlaw had been in a jovial mood since leaving DeLamar, enjoying needling his captor, but as night drew on and the stars appeared he began to wax nostalgic. It rapidly passed from boring to sickening to Raider, but he let him prattle on without comment. Any talk was preferable to insults and argument.

"I've made lotsa mistakes in my life, I have for fair, but one thing I can be peacock proud o': when I die and hasta go to heaven and stand before God's judgment seat, I'll be able to hold my head up with pride for the grand job I done raisin' my two young-uns."

"Oh for Chrissakes."

"Stop your foul mouth! I'm dead serious. I'm talkin' 'bout my only flesh and blood."

"Whatever happened to their mother?"

"Tragedy o' my life, that woman. She was useless as a pump 'thout a handle and dizzy in the head to boot. She runned off, left me flat when they was mere tads. I raised 'em by myself, I did. Her name was Clotilda. She was addled."

"She couldn't have been too addled if she ran away from you."

"With a horse swapper. He was twice't her age. I chased 'em clear across Missouri. Fin'ly caught up with 'em."

"Whatja do, shoot 'em?"

He stiffened. He looked genuinely pained. His eyes took on a sheepish look.

Raider decided that it was exactly what he'd done. "You're a blue wonder, Ira. You're special you are, special rotten."

"If you knowed the pain, the ang'ish that woman put me through, the grief and sufferin', and leavin' me with two young babies barely eight and ten, you wouldn't be so quick to cast stones o' rebuke."

"Horseshit! Knowin' you, you didn't even bring 'em up. I'll bet you dumped 'em off on your sister Rose o' Sharon Elsie or Aunt Ola and Uncle Anson over in Louisiana."

Again Pickett's reaction announced he'd hit the nail squarely. "You're a vicious bastard, you know that?"

"And you're the father o' the world, you are. You haven't got a spark o' decency in your whole miserable body. Don't care 'bout anybody but yourself. Small wonder nobody cares 'bout you."

"Ha! We'll see, Razorback. You'll see what Jason and Caleb think o' their pappy. They'll show ya by their deeds, bless their dear lovin' and loyal hearts. If you got prayers to say you'd best start sayin' 'em. Sand's runnin' outta your glass. Brother, you are as good as dead."

Raider was crouching over the fire. Without thinking, he straightened and looked around. He strained his ears. He could hear the murmur of the wind and the night, but nothing else—no coyote, no horses, nothing for a mile in every direction. Nevertheless, experience cautioned him that his imagination could conjure up any sound, and at

times like these it could nag him insideously. He resolved
to make a special effort to keep it in check, but his rising
and looking about was not lost on Pickett. He continued to
stir the ashes of worry. If he let Pickett get to him, Raider
thought, in time he'd have him jumping at shadows, cursing the dark, and expecting Jason and Caleb to jump from
behind every rock and clump of sagebrush.

"You want coffee?"

"Ha! Coffee's the last thing you're thinkin' 'bout right
now. They're comin' loaded for bear. With rifles. They
won't even have to come close 'nough for you to see 'em
for 'em to shoot you dead. That's the scary part. They're
comin', or are they 'head o' us? Whata ya think, Razorback? Will they come by dark or at sunup or blaze o' noon
or afternoon, comin' outta the sun, blindin' you so's you
can't see past the front o' your eyeballs?

"I know, they'll wait till we're up in the Independence
Mountains. They'll bushwhack you. They'll put twelve
slugs into you before you can get out your iron. Then it's
off to Californy for the three o' us!"

"No coffee."

"You just offered me! Gimme some!"

Raider sipped from the cup and handed it to him.

"Jesus! Tastes like sheep dip!"

"I wouldn't know, but I'm sure you do."

They ate dry biscuits and beef jerky and finished what
remained in the coffeepot. He was right, thought Raider, it
did taste foul, close to rancid. He decided the pot needed
breaking in. After he restored the utensils to his saddlebags
he attended to their horses then set about tying Pickett's
wrists behind his back.

"What are you doin'? Tie me front. I sleeps on my
back."

"You'll sleep on your side. You'll like it for a change.
You'll be able to see the scorpions comin'."

"Bullshit! They's no scorpions this far north."

"You don't think so?"

"Arizona, Texas, not Idaho. It's bullshit."

"You're wrong, I've seen 'em clear up to the border. I was bit by one above the snowline in Montana timber country."

"Liar!"

'Okay, only you don't wanta lie on your back. On your back you won't see 'em comin', you'll only feel 'em when they get there."

"Liar. Liar!"

Good, he thought, now the boot's on our foot. Now you've got something to prey on *your* mind tonight.

CHAPTER FIFTEEN

Raider awoke, sat up, and looked around warily. Clouds
blotted out the stars and moon, and the wind had come up,
strewing sand about, bending the grasses where the horses
stood, curling down into the dry wash, and ripping fire
from the glowing embers. Pickett was snoring, lying on his
side with no scorpions about.

A noise had awakened Raider, a sound intruding on the
vast and weighty silence capturing their surroundings. So
advised his instincts, but what it was precisely he had no
idea. He braced himself with one arm, closed his eyes,
waited for the wind to die, and listened intently.

There it was again, a loud click. No mistake, no imagination. He stiffened, his hand straying to his gun. It was
the sound of a cartridge being pushed into the receiver. He
flattened. Again the wind dove into the wash and flapped
the front of his hat brim. He tore his hat off and sat it
beside him. Very slowly, he began to pull himself forward,
passing the cook fire, ascending the grade to the rim of the

wash. He stopped with it just above his head. He crabbed sideways until his body was parallel to the rim. He glanced back at Pickett, who was still snoring. He raised his head slightly, carefully, for a look.

A rifle cracked, and a second one, the sounds so close they were almost simultaneous. The first shot grazed the side of his head, the second slammed into it just above his right eye. It felt like a nail driven home with a single blow of the hammer. It snapped his head back sharply. It stung. His brain exploded, his skull shattered. Fragments of bone and bloody bits of brain flew in every direction. He had begun to turn his head when the bullet struck, intending to swing about and look back at Pickett a second time. Hit, he still did so. And saw pieces of his skull and brain strike and splatter against Pickett's face. He woke, his eyes unsealed, He gaped. He leered.

Raider woke, sat bolt upright, fumbled for his gun, found it, and started to draw, but stopped with it half out. He was drenched with sweat; his shirt was wringing wet. He fought to catch his breath, but a steel collar was around his neck, shrinking, tightening, choking him. His hands flew to his throat. He tired to pull the collar loose to get air into him; there was no collar. Fear was the collar, a steel ring forged by his imagination, nurtured by Pickett's threats of ambush. He looked over at him. He was looking straight at Raider, grinning devilishly, his eyes wide, seeing nothing. He was snoring. He was asleep.

Raider shook off his fear and sucked his lungs full of the cold, sweet air. He thought about the recent past, the last forty-eight hours, and now about what lay ahead. Nearly 150 miles to go, and the mountains would be the most treacherous phase. If Pickett's sons were to intercept them —and he had no doubt but that they would—it would be in the mountains.

He thought about Lloyd, Blodgett and the others, all dead now, and Doc, the lone survivor lying with a bullet in his brisket. His condition was still critical; if the operation wasn't touchy Von Zell wouldn't be putting it off until his general condition improved, improving his chances.

He thought about the small piece of eternity that was his own life. What a discouragingly fragile thing it was in this business, how vulnerable, such easy prey to violence, to accident. If you buy and sell shoes for a living your chances of getting shot are practically nil, Doc always said, if you buy and sell gunplay. . .

Again he looked over at the sleeping Pickett. He had turned over on his other side, removing his face from Raider's sight, but his smirk was no doubt still there, put on to taunt and unnerve him, to upset him. That was its sole purpose.

He was a piece of work, was Mr. Ira Pickett—a fighting machine, a two-legged wild animal without conscience, without scruple, without even a hint of the behavioral values that distinguish a human being from a furry brute. An even better comparison was a buzzard—ugly, disgusting-looking, blood-loving, carrion-eating spawn of hell.

Raider swore under his breath. He had fallen asleep. Upon lying down, he had steeled his mind against sleep, vowing to keep at least one eye open, and both ears. He had slept well the night before, the sleep of the dead. He ached all over, but had no real, serious pain, apart from his jaw where he'd lost the tooth. Beef jerky was not the best thing he could eat to restore his lost blood, but he'd had a huge breakfast and lunch and all in all felt okay, not weak. How, he wondered, did Pickett feel? Each had given the other a sound thrashing. Pickett had ridden to the shack, not been draped over a horse's withers; but, all things considered, they had suffered pretty equal abuse. But the older man certainly didn't look it, and probably didn't feel it. His nose had been shattered and probably other bones, but you'd never know it to see him walk, mount a horse, and ride.

"Son of a bitch isn't human!"

Raider yawned. Unlike in his nightmare, the heavens

had not clouded over. The stars still pulsated brightly. The North Star hovered only slightly to the right of a straight line up from the outside top corner of the Big Dipper, indicating four in the morning. It would be dawn soon. They would rise, eat, and start out. He planned a 100-mile day. That this optimism tallied with their horses' plans for the distance they intended to cover was doubtful, but when night returned, hopefully they would be up into the Independence Mountains with still light enough left to locate a cave. If he got lucky and found one with an open space in front of it he could litter the space in an arc around the mouth with dry grass so that anyone sneaking up in the darkness would betray their arrival by the crunching underfoot. As primitive as it was, it did work. He knew, he'd used it before.

Pickett awoke looking disgustingly refreshed, Raider reflected, studying him. He sat up, stretched, beamed, and started the day with his first demand.

"Untie me, for Chrissakes, I can't piss with my wrists like this."

Raider untied him. As he did so Pickett made a point off staring fixedly at his six-gun in its holster.

"Go for it, Ira, I dare you."

"Why should I? I don't have to, don't have to lift a finger. Jace and Caleb'll rescue me and finish you off before lunchtime. What's for breakfast?"

"For you, your bridle and a cuppa sand."

"Hurry up and make the coffee."

"You hate my coffee."

"I was just pullin' your leg. Shake it up, I'm hungry."

They ate. Pickett resumed sketching mind pictures of Raider's downfall.

Raider let him babble without commenting until it came time to start out. "They'd better make their move today. At the rate we're goin' we'll be in Elko by mid-afternoon tomorrow."

"They know when to make their move. They're watchin' us right now."

"You see 'em?"

"Don't have to, I know they're there. And Asa and Willis McColl with 'em. How do you want it, Razorback? In the head? The brisket? Maybe you prefers hangin'. There's them that does. Not me. When I gets it I want it quick. One in the heart's good 'nough for this old boy. Course it'll never happen. I'll never hang neither. Ha, not this time, we won't get within ten mile o' Elko before they show up and cash you in. No sir, I plan to die in a featherbed at ninety-eight with my sons, my grandsons, and my great-grandsons standin' round mournin' and in tears. I'm gonna be a legend, I am."

"Can I have your autograph?"

"You're dead."

"Not yet."

"Tomorrow's it for you. Hisst, what's that?" Raider tensed. "Fooledja! 'Snothin'. Look at you, Chrissakes, you ain't been awake twenny minutes and already you're startin' to sweat. Can't be the sun. I'm not. It's your fear. Real rough grindin' fear does that to a body, eats you alive, your skin feels like it's on fire, your guts boilin' inside."

Raider grunted and poured the rest of the coffee out on the ground.

"Hey, what the hell you do that for? I woulda drunk it."

"Oh, sorry, I thought two cups was 'nough."

"Vicious bastard! I'm gonna report you to the 'thorities for abusin' and torturin' me when we get in. I may be your pris'ner, but I'm human, I got rights. When we get in . . ."

"What are you talkin' about? You changed your mind? No Jace? No Caleb? No ambush? No rescue? Whatta ya think, did they lose their way? What are they, wanderin' round back up to Duck Valley lookin' for us?"

"You're funny like a busted leg, you know that? Laugh all you like. He who laughs last laughs best!"

"Hey, hey! Shake your right hand there. Hard! Shake

off that scorpion 'fore it bites ya!"

"Ahhhh!" Pickett shook his hand violently, recoiling, glaring.

Raider laughed and laughed.

CHAPTER SIXTEEN

By morning of the second full day traveling Raider was so exhausted he had to force his eyelids to stay open and his body to stay upright. Once more, for perhaps the twentieth time, he had fallen asleep. Tension was grinding him down to a nub. It was no longer anything Pickett said; he had long since give up paying any attention to his rambling threats. It was all worry of his own devising. He had tried on fear, it fit, and he kept it on; there seemed no way of divesting himself of it. His imagination was wholeheartedly committed to it, and much as he loathed the prospect he concluded he would have to live with it till Elko. The worst of it was it was so obvious. Pickett saw it and needled him mercilessly.

"We'll be seeing the Indies b'fore noon, Razorback, want a little tip?"

"Don't you ever get tired o' talkin'?"

"Never. Not as long as I got somebody'll listen. You sure like to. The tip is this: don't try crossin' them, go roun'. Cut left now, head east, and you'll skirt the north

152

end. It's only 'bout sixty mile outta the way, but safer. Goin' over 'em like you're plannin' is suicide."

Raider looked at the horses. To anyone watching him— to Pickett, for instance—he was weighing the alternative.

"Think 'bout it."

"I already have, even before we left DeLamar. No go. We've pushed the horses too hard gettin' this far to add that long a stretch."

"Its' gotta be even harder for 'em goin' over the top."

"No it won't. We'll rest every half hour, and if we come to a real steep trail, maybe an hour or more. We'll let them set the pace for us."

"You're makin' a mistake. Come nightfall we'll be stuck up top. The dark sneaks up on ya fast in the mountains this time o' year. The las' thing you want is to be stuck up there after dark. That's a sure-fire open invitation to Jace, Caleb, and the boys."

"Tell me somethin'."

"Shoot."

"Ever stop to think what could happen if the kids do show? That I'd have to gun 'em down before your very eyes? You'd stand there helpless and watch 'em die. Some terrible sight for a dotin' father, not one but both sons dyin' right before your eyes."

Pickett laughed, but thinly, with an all-too-evident edge of anxiety to it. Raider suddenly felt like he was holding the sure winning hand in a high-stakes game of draw. He couldn't lose. The harder he pressed, the more he raised, the more he'd win.

"What then, Ira? What do we do, just leave 'em where they fall? We don't have a shovel, nothin' to dig with. I expect we'll just have to cover 'em up with rocks, maybe get a couple sticks and make crosses to mark 'em."

"Shut up!"

"I wouldn't hesitate to kill 'em. I'd have to. It's either them or me, right? After you, that is. You're first in line. They shoot at me, I shoot you. That'll shake 'em up,

they'll be so shocked they'll be bound to do somethin'
jackass, like jump up yellin', cussin', go wild. And make it
easy for me—"

"Vicious bastard! You got no heart at all. I bet you ain't
even a Christian. You ever go to church? Ever read the
Bible? I read it all the time. I could quote whole passages.
'The Lord preserveth all those what love him; but all the
wicked will he dee-stroy.' That's from Proverbs. Or the
Psalms. One or t'other. Don't matter. I knows just 'bout
the whole entire Bible by heart. My gran'pappy was a
stump preacher."

"You told me."

"I never did tell ya 'bout Jason and Caleb. Two o' the
finest young-uns ever to breathe the good Lord's fresh air
and feel His warm sunlight on their han'some cheeks."

"They look just like you. Jace does, anyway. I haven't
seen the other."

"Both look like me."

"Ugly as sin."

Raider's head was down, his eyes on the cook fire.
Pickett leaped, pouncing on him, knocking him over, but
as Raider fell he reached for his gun. He got it out as he
rolled over, got Pickett in his sights, both arms upraised,
his face black with anger, tensed and ready to spring again.
The gun froze him. He slowly straightened, lowered his
arms, and glowered fiercely.

"You don't talk like that 'bout my boys. You never say
that again, never! You do and I'll kill ya!"

"They're ugly as sin."

He went wild. Raider fired. The slug flew past Pickett's
ear, stopping him in his tracks.

"The next one'll push your nose to the back o' your
head and I'll be draggin' you in with the rope. Come on,
come at me."

He gave it up. "Quit the goddamn horseplay and get out
the grub, Chrissakes, I'm hungry as a bear."

•   •   •

Around nine in the morning the Independence Mountains began to define their presence against the burning sky.

"There they be!" Pickett exclaimed. "What's it gonna be, go roun' like a sensible man or cross like a ig'orant asshole?"

Raider said nothing. Over the past two hours he had been speculating on the possibilities that would be awaiting them in the mountains. Neither Asa Hudlin or Willis McColl were within 300 miles, he decided, but the boys were probably up ahead lying in wait for them. He put himself in their boots. Chasing out of the pocket after Asa and Willis on Ira's orders, what had they run into? What was out there but Shoshones? Had they been butchered? Were all four bodies now lying in draws or ravines? It had been some surprise emerging with Pickett to find no one, nothing, not even a stray pony. Had the outlaws and Indians gone upward instead of down? There'd been time enough before he and Pickett came out for all to clear out, but he hadn't expected that they would. The more he thought about it, the more it seemed possible that Jace and Caleb were dead, and still lying where they'd been struck down. They'd never left the Owyhees.

He had marched Pickett to DeLamar and a jail cell. If his sons *had* survived and come back to look for him, failing to find either of them, what else could they assume but that he'd gotten the upper hand and taken him away to jail? Of course there was no way they could have known then about Abington's being killed in the action on the Murphy road. But they certainly realized *he* knew that the sheriff wasn't to be trusted, that if their father was to be jailed it wouldn't be in Silver City but DeLamar. He'd been lodged there overnight and into the next morning. So why hadn't they come nosing around?

They were dead. Had to be. Didn't *have* to, but it seemed a good bet. Just not good enough to stake his life on. Still, dealing Hudlin and McColl out of the game helped some. It halved the firepower against him.

Again he considered circling the northern end of the mountains instead of crossing them. If he changed his mind at this point, though, he'd have to backtrack a good ten miles when he cut east. They'd come that far down.

"We're crossin' and that's that," he muttered.

"You say somethin'?"

"Nothin'. You must be hearin' things."

In less than two hours they reached the foothills and began to ascend. The sun seemed hotter today than yesterday.

Raider took off his hat and wiped his head and face with his bandanna.

"Murd'rous hot, ain't it? My horse needs water," Pickett said. He started to pull up.

"Both canteens are almost empty. Keep goin'. We'll try and find a stream."

'You won't find no stream this late in the summer. Not here."

"You know these mountains—"

"I know my nose. I can smell water six mile away, and I can't smell nothin' roun' here."

Two breaths later water could be heard gushing close by.

The Independence Mountains were similar to the Owyhees in the sparseness of their vegetation, their sharply rising, smoothly planed stone, their many fissures and crevices and tortuously twisting narrow trail. It zigzagged upward into the brutal sun. Raider scanned the heights apprehensively, tensing in spite of himself until he was stiff as steel. And tired, stifling yawn after yawn with his fist. Pickett, riding four lengths ahead, could not see him save in his mind's eye. It saw an accurate picture.

"Worried sick, ain'tcha, Razorback? You should be. They're up there." He raised his arm, waved, and yelled their names.

"Shut up!"

"Here we come!"

"I said shut up!" Raider heeled his horse. It lunged forward, bringing him up alongside Pickett. He grabbed Pickett's shoulder, squeezing hard, forcing him to cringe. "One more word, one sound and I'll bust you one."

"Just sendin' up a fatherly greetin'..." He pulled up and stopped.

Raider did likewise.

A pebble came bouncing down, striking a rock, arcing, falling, striking another, the action repeated, repeated. It finally dropped into a crevice and lodged there.

"Hee hee hee hee hee. What'd I tell ya? Was I right? Stones don't come bouncin' down less'n they're started by somethin'. By somebody, right? Right?"

"Keep goin'. No, stop!"

"Make up your mind."

"Get down."

"What for?"

"Do like I say."

Raider continued to scan the summit warily. He had his gun out and cocked. A Cooper's hawk came floating effortlessly over the ridge and into view, its striped breast and banded tail's colors indistinguishable in the sun's glare, but its short, rounded wings and long, round tail clearly identifiable.

Pickett had dismounted.

Raider, too, got down. "Keep goin' afoot," he ordered.

The first shot rang off a rock less than a foot from Raider's head to his left. He ducked instinctively and fired back.

Pickett cowered, hunching down into a ball and chortling gleefully. "Git him, Jace! Caleb! Blow 'is head off!"

A flurry of shots sent Raider scurrying up behind Pickett, his momentum carrying him squarely into him, bowling him over. Raider backed behind a convenient ledge just in time. Shots rained against the rock.

"You snotnoses, you hear me? I'm gonna show. With him. With my gun back o' his head. One more shot from you and he's dead. Y'hear me?" He looked out at Pickett, who was still cowering, his forearms crossed over his head protectively. He was no longer laughing. The color was rapidly draining from the cheek Raider could see.

Raider reached and set his muzzle so hard against Pickett's head he yelped and drew left.

"Hold still, and start prayin' they heard and can see. At the count o' three, get up, straighten up to your full height, and raise your hands. One . . . two . . . three."

Both rose. Raider held his breath. His thudding heart counted fifteen beats. There was no movement above and no sound above or below save the breeze. Overhead the hawk had vanished.

"I guess that's that, Ira. Tough luck they can't hit the side of a barn. Get back on your horse and keep goin'. It's less'n a hundred yards to the top."

"That's that your ass. They're just feelin' you out, that's all, toyin' with ya. Ha, they can see you clear as day, whilst you can't see nothin'. Glare's on their side. You're a dead man. Dead!"

Raider tightened his grip on his gun. "Shut up."

"It's a true fac', it's—"

Another volley came singing down, this time left and right, indicating they had separated and were working their way toward crossfire positions. The thought flew through Raider's mind as he dove from his horse, landing between rocks, a slug winging his upper arm just under the shoulder, ripping the fabric of his shirt, laying a red finger of blood across the tear. They continued firing as he examined it. It wasn't until he was done, having decided the wound was nothing, that he realized he had dropped his gun in diving for safety. There it lay in the middle of the path behind his horse. Sunlight struck the barrel and bounced off it.

The shooting stopped, ending with a single tardy shot. Raider swiped at his flesh wound, bringing his fingers back down gleaming crimson.

"Assholes. Can't hit the side of a barn."

He waited. He could hear no scrambling up the path,

but he was unable to see, since the rock effectively blocked his view. How was Pickett faring? he wondered. In spite of his curiosity, he didn't dare peer around the rock. Not yet. Instead he eased around the other way, distancing himself further from the path, only to find that there the rocks rose sharply ahead of him, making it impossible to see anything.

"Ira?"

"Yeah?"

"You okay?"

"Hee hee hee. He's wond'rin' 'bout me. If that ain't a caution. Worried 'bout *me!* I'm proper fine, Razorback. Fitter'n a fiddle. Why wouldn't I be? What about you? You wounded? Must be."

Raider did not answer him. Pickett prattled on. Raider moved a few steps further from the path, stopped, and listened, but could hear nothing above. He finally made his way back to very near his horse, pausing a moment before venturing from behind his cover. Then, crouching and steeling himself, he emerged. To his surprise Pickett had remounted.

I told you on foot. Get down!"

"Why? I ain't in no danger. Just 'cause you are, why should I have to walk? You got to, so's you won't have so far to fall when you're shot."

Incensed by Pickett's contrariness, upset over his wound, physically and emotionally drained, fed up with Pickett's leer and endless taunting, unnerved by the precariousness of the situation, Raider cursed, snatched up his gun, and fired. The bullet skinned by Pickett's cheek and ricocheted off a rock behind him. He erupted in laughter, the echo bouncing off the rocks above. It signaled more shooting. Again Raider dove to safety, this time hanging on to his gun. He righted himself and, with his back against a rock, reloaded.

Keeping so low his chin nearly touched the ground, he crept back to the path and looked up it. Pickett was where he'd left him, still in his saddle, his back to him. But no sooner did Raider's mind confirm the impression on his eyes then Pickett began tilting backwards, falling over his horse's rump, somersaulting, landing in the path on his back, his spine cracking sickeningly.

Dead center his forehead was a single red button.

CHAPTER SEVENTEEN

Doc lay still, surrounding the bullet in his chest, breathing tentatively for fear of starting up the pain again, as had become his habit. He was sweating, wondering. The door opened. Dr. Von Zell came in, poking at an upper tooth with one end of his glasses. In his free hand he carried a clipboard with yellow pages filled with scribbling. He looked as if he hadn't slept in a week.

"Doc," he began. He frowned. "Vhere did you ged dot name? Are you a doctor?"

"Nickname. I sometimes sell homeopathic medicines as a respectable cover for investigating."

"Respegtable, you say? Vot's respegtable about homeopadic medizines? Dere in a glass mit schnake oil. Hey, ve god der vinal vigures on der big party the other nide. A hundred dirty-dree dead, a hundred eighty vounded."

"Good Lord."

"Bod zides zuffered heavily. I undershtand, howeffer, dot ze oudlaws haff pretty much cleared oud, zo zumting good has gum oud uff id after all. A vederal marshal has daken ofer in Zilver Zity. Dot in idzelf vas enough to zend dem packing. How do you veel?"

"The same."

"I've decided to go in after id."

"I thought you wanted to put it off a few days."

"Too risky. Invegtion. As I zaid before, id's nod going to be easy, bud leaving id in . . ." He shook his head. "Id's snugged just under der right ventricle. Tank Gott vor der pericardium; id's a tough, vibrous sac zurrounds der heart, brotects it. Vidout id . . ."

"Let's get it over with."

"Don't be in such a rush. Giff me den minutes. Mrs. Hennis vill giff you chlorovorm. I von't lie to you, my vriend, id's in dere very deep. Exzizing it vill be murder . . . I mean . . ." Doc managed a grin. "But ve'll ged id oud."

"How long will I be recuperating?"

"Blease, virst tings virst. Reguperation ve dalk aboud tomorrow."

If there is one, mused Doc ruefully. Von Zell left. Doc sighed and considered his situation. Von Zell didn't fool him for a minute. He wasn't worried about the bullet being lodged too close to the heart. There was no danger to the heart, the danger would be from bleeding. Doc would bleed like a stuck pig. The problem would be how to keep it under control while probing deep enough to get at the slug. A pity his body, the bed, the room weren't in Peter Bent Brigham in Boston or some other reputable hospital in a large city. With all sorts of modern equipment at the surgeon's disposal, efficient assistants, absolute control over infection, proper lighting.

Von Zell seemed competent, only that was it: "seemed." Doc had no way of knowing whether he was or not. He certainly had to be experienced in removing slugs. What doctor west of the Mississippi wasn't expert in that line? What were his chances? Doc wondered. Fifty-fifty? Better? Not that good? Why was he sweating so? Did it signal infection? Was it already raging through him, with the pain of it soon to arrive? Probably not. Von Zell would have opened him up two days ago if that worried him. He had given him nearly three days to recoup his strength, to build him up for the knife, but now that they had elapsed he didn't *feel* any stronger, and his steadily mounting anxiety certainly didn't increase his strength.

He had been operated on before four times: his appendix when he was only twelve, and it was removed without a hitch back in Massachusetts, the other three occasions when bullets were removed (not counting at least a dozen surface wounds wherein the slug practically fell out of its own weight). Only one of the three approached the seriousness of this. That bullet had lodged deep in his thigh. The doctor had no anesthetic, had given him two shots of bourbon and a tongue depressor to clamp between his teeth. Doc had suffered horribly and bled like two pigs. At least this time they would put him under.

His hand wandered to his wound, hovering just above it, hesitatant to actually touch it. He pictured the slug lying at a slight angle inside and the probe approaching it from above. Blood spurted up around it as it dug deeper and deeper. And, God in heaven, *passed the slug,* and dug and dug, and bled and bled . . .

Von Zell's ten minutes must be down to five by now. He began to count seconds. They arrived early, thirty-two counts before he reached zero. Von Zell's friendly smile could only be described as strained. Mrs. Hennis didn't even try. She looked worried to death.

For close to four hours, by his rough reckoning, Raider sat behind his rock waiting for Pickett's sons to make their next move. It was close to two in the afternoon when he decided they would not. They'd probably pulled out. No, that was wishful thinking and an obvious trap, one to be scrupulously avoided. Did they realize they'd killed their father? No. If they did they would have sent up a howl capable of shaking down every nugget of rubble along the ridge. Whether they realized it or not, why had they stopped shooting? Could they be out of ammunition? No. Another obvious trap he refused to blunder into.

Were they sitting up there waiting for him to make *his* move? That seemed likely. Their father lay where he'd fallen, on his back, his eyes wide and staring blankly at the sun. His horse stood quietly, gently swishing her tail. In this heat both their horses would be needing water soon, despite having filled up earlier in the day down below.

For the tenth time he checked his gun. And decided he would play it their way. He would go after them. If they were still sitting above him, and he couldn't for a moment make himself believe they were not, they wouldn't expect him to try a frontal approach. They'd be delighted if he did, but wouldn't expect it. Which left one side or the other.

Or from the rear. Not a bad idea. He stood up and shading his eyes, studied the terrain to his left, then in the opposite direction. A narrow pathway twisted down the slope to his left as he faced the base of the mountains. It dropped a good fifty yards before curving around one of the few boulders in sight that could be described as roughly round and started upward again. Holstering his gun, he loped down the path, around the boulder, and started upward. The path ran diagonally sharply right to a saddle. It was located perhaps a quarter mile to the right of the head of the path on which Ira lay, but anyone up top had the benefit of an unimpeded view of it, so that if he tried for it, once he got there he'd either have to chance bellying over to veer off even further right to get over the top without being seen.

This he did to play it safe. Even so, he expected a hail of bullets every step of the way. Reaching the other side, he could look off in the distance and see Elko squatting by the railroad tracks with the glistening ribbon that was the Humboldt River stretching east of it. Pickett was right about one thing, *he* never would see Elko. But he'd get there.

"I promise you that, Ira. You, me, and your two clown sons."

Gun in hand, he started down the opposite side. If they spotted him, he thought anxiously, now was the time to open up. He had virtually no cover to his left and only an occasional outcropping to the right that in a pinch he could dive behind. Coming to a stretch of ledge, he deserted the path and started around it, coming up the other side and beginning his ascent to the ridge. The sun, now positioned off his left shoulder, was starting down the sky. He had moved about twenty-five yards upward, picking his way carefully through the rocks, keenly aware that if he slipped, the noise would surely catch their attention and bring him the barrage he dreaded, when his foot struck a stone the size of a cantaloupe, sending it rumbling down and triggering a flurry of shots. One knocked his hat off. Another grazed his wound, releasing fresh blood and setting him cursing as he hurled himself behind cover.

He waited a long moment, then ventured around the other side of his rock, sneaked a look, spied a hat, and fired. The echo from his second shot was still bouncing about the rocks when a scream went up, lifting, splitting the sky like lightning and dying as quickly as it had raised. Again he looked. One of them, he couldn't tell which, lay draped over a rock, smoking rifle in hand, his hat deserting his head and bouncing merrily downward.

"Bastard! Sumabitch!" The other rose up blasting, firing blindly, wildly, emptying his rifle, flinging it away, recklessly leaning down to retrieve his brother's from his lifeless grasp.

Two-handing his gun, Raider squinted careful aim, pulled, and shot him through the hand. An unearthly screech rent the air. Raider stepped forth, fired again, and froze him where he lay just above his brother.

"Ya killed him! Ya killed Jace!"

"And you killed your father."

"You're a damn liar! Where is he? What ya done with

him, Pinkerton bastard. Killer! Murderin' slime!"

"Shut up and come down with your hands up."

"I won't! I can't! I'm hurtin' terrible bad. I'm dyin'. I know it. I feels it."

"I'll blow your head off, and I guarantee you'll feel that if you don't do like you're told. Move!"

Caleb came stumbling down, gripping his wrist low in front of him, his wounded hand down, carrying on as if undergoing the tortures of the damned. "Bullet went clean through. I'm gonna lose my hand, I am. Bastard, murderin' slime!"

He came within twenty feet. Raider could now clearly see the site of entry. The bullet had driven through the fleshy portion at the vee formed by the bases of thumb and forefinger. The muscle would never the same, but it wasn't nearly as serious as he was making it out to be. He was lucky, an inch lower and it would have shattered bone.

"Jace is dead, Jace is dead."

"Your father's dead too, Caleb."

"Liar!"

"He is."

"Liar, liar, liar, liar!"

"Cross my heart. One o' you did it."

"We didn' neither, you did! You shot Pa too, murderin' slime! Pig! Bastard!"

"Shut up! Jesus, I've had his mouth all the way down from DeLamar, I'll be goddamned if I'll put up with yours the rest o' the way. Shut up and stay shut up. Drop your hands and turn round. We're goin' up and get your horses and him. We'll go back down the other side and get your father. Then we're goin' on to Elko."

"What for?"

"I'll tell you on the way. Does the Southern Pacific ring a bell? Let's go."

CHAPTER EIGHTEEN

"Will he make it?"

"You alvays ask me dot und I alvays giff you der zame anzer, zo why ask?"

"So much blood, like a bursting pipe."

"I knew dere vould be, but I neffer dreamed vot was inzide dere."

"Two bullets."

"Mit only vun point uff endry. Id vus just luck I vound bod."

"He never said anything about being shot twice there, did he?"

"No. He must nod haff realized he vas."

"How could he not?"

"Zearch me. He could haff been unconscious ven dey vent in or in all der eggcitement zimply vailed to notice. He took a bullet in der leg, too, remember, maybe dot distracted him. Two bullets und only vun hole, dot is amazing."

"He's a very lucky man you found both."

"Lucky I vas lucky."

"You're exhausted. You shoud lie down."

"If I do I von't get up vor dree days. Who's next?"

Doc heard them at a great distance, as if they were standing whispering at the far end of an enormous empty room. It struck him that he was not dead, not alive, but suspended over the bottomless abyss separating the two. Mrs. Hennis answered the doctor, but he couldn't make out what she said, her voice pulling even further away, out of hearing range. He felt no pain; he felt nothing below his neck. He did feel relief. Despite Von Zell's reluctance to speculate on his chances, he assured himself that he *had* made it.

Raider placed Caleb at the head of the line. He held the reins of his brother's horse; his father's was tied behind it. Raider brought up the rear. They stopped just above the foothills at the same spring he and Ira had stopped by earlier. All the way down the slope he wouldn't take his eyes off Ira, draped ignominiously over his horse, his wrists tied to his ankles to prevent his slipping from his saddle. A piece of work indeed, one of a kind, perhaps—when Raider reflected on his past twelve years of experience, the worst he had ever locked horns with. Without question the toughest for his age. Thief, robber, murderer of many, including his own wife, the mother of his sons. Claimant to just about every crime in the black register and guilty of pushing his sons off the straight and narrow, turning them to his way with the result that one was now dead and other faced hanging.

Raider had never known anyone (and he had known most of the worst infesting and infecting the territories) as determinedly contemptible as Ira. Nor anyone so bad and so colorful at once. He was that. The man had had a personality like a fireworks display, as loud, as eye-dazzling, entertaining, energetic, explosive . . . His mouth never tired, his stock of sarcasm and insults never gave out, lies tumbled from his lips without let up, he exhausted the senses.

Raider would miss him, already did. Neither of his boys had his personality, his wit and flair. Yes, he was colorful, fascinating, even—God help him for thinking it—appealing in his bizarre and twisted way. Raider craned his neck to study his craggy profile, his head bobbing lightly with the horse's every step. Ira, Ira. His bragging words came back as hollow, as meaningless as they had when he'd uttered them. He'd never get to God's judgment seat to hear the Almighty praise him for bringing his sons up so well; he'd never see Heaven. He was already headed in the opposite direction.

"I sure pity Old Scratch. He'll have his hands full when you show up. You'll turn his Hell wrongside to, upside down, inside out. You'll have him lookin' for the first door out. You'll have the place in a uproar, fault-findin', tellin' everybody how to run things, what they're doin' wrong, how to stoke the fires, how to deal out the sulphur and brimstone. God and the angels don't know how lucky they are, what they'll be missin'. Old Scratch should call up and tell 'em. If they knew they'd fall down on their knees every one and offer up a special prayer of thanks and gratefulness for bein' spared you. The poor Devil, he may just toss in the sponge and retire, turn the whole shebang over to you, pack his bags and leave. I sure would if I were him."

The sun was lowering over the ridge of the Independence Mountains when they came plodding into Elko, attracting all eyes. They were halfway through town when the door to the sheriff's office on the left just past Arnican's Drugs & Sundries opened and a familiar figure came out. Raider recognized Marshal Tutweiler. He watched the marshall stare, his eyes taking in Caleb in the lead, move to Jason, to Ira, and settle on Raider and brighten as he recognized him.

Raider recalled he was from Beowawe in Eureka County to the west. What was he doing in Elko? Was business so slow he could travel around calling on his fellow peace officers?

"I'll be jiggered!" Tutweiler exclaimed in greeting.

It brought another man to the door. He was tall, dark, and roughly half the marshal's sixty years. He was hatless and held a knife and a half-whittled figure of some sort. At first sight Raider liked his face. He had a no-nonsense set to his jaw and dead serious eyes.

Tutweiler came over to Ira's horse as they pulled up and bent to examine his face. "This the ringleader?"

"Ira Pickett," said Raider. "Chief scalawag."

"Where's the others?"

"Scattered and dead. Mostly dead. He throttled two in the cell next to his in DeLamar. The live one there's his son Caleb, the other, son Jason. Real active family."

"Where's your partner?"

"He's gettin' the lead picked outta him up in Murphy. That's a whole other story. He'll be okay."

Marshal Tutweiler introduced him to Sheriff Merrill Conklin.

"The marshal told me about the holdup over near Battle Mountain. You do realize that's Humboldt County, Ben Hartline's bailiwick. How come you didn't take this bunch over to Winnemucca?"

"What the hell's the difference? It's the Southern Pacific's case. Railroad cases spread all over the map. And it'll be the same judge here as there. It's all Nevada. Look, you don't want this load, send over to Winnemucca and have somebody come and fetch it and haul it to there, I don't care. I come a long way, I'm beat, starved for a decent meal, thirsty as a goat . . . brother, for all I care you can turn him loose and toss the dead ones down the closest dry well."

"Don't get upset," said Conklin hastily, and suppressed a grin. "Just asking. I don't mind taking them. I would like to ask you a couple questions, though. Leonard, take Jesse James there inside and lock him up, would you?"

"You'll be lockin' up the wrong man, Sheriff. He's the

one you want. He shot Pa and Jace in cold blood. Coldest-blooded murderer I've ever saw. He's the one should hang."

Caleb redirected his harangue to the crowd that had started to assemble. Tutweiler got him down and pushed him inside.

"Heartless murderer, that's what he is! He is!"

Conklin politely advised the curious to go about their business. They did so reluctantly.

"How did you happen to shoot him?" asked Conklin.

"I didn't. One of his kids did."

"His own son?"

"You don't see anybody else, do you? It was up in the mountains. They were shootin' at me and hit him. It figures. Both were wilder'n wet hens on a trigger."

The sheriff was studying Ira's face. "Dead center the forehead. You trying to say it was accidental?"

Raider scratched the side of his head. "Now you mention it, I wonder. They sure had clear 'nough sight o' him. And when whichever shot him did they didn't react, not right then. Jesus."

"It was deliberate."

"I don't know."

"Wouldn't be the first time a hostage was killed."

"Their own father. It's crazy."

"How'd they get along with him.?"

Raider shrugged. "All right, I guess. He'd jump on 'em for every little thing, like most fathers, but it didn't seem to bother either. When I *told* 'em he'd been shot they did put up a howl. Like it was a big surprise. But they coulda seen easy. The big delayed reaction coulda been for my benefit, I suppose. I don't know, Sheriff, I really can't say. Really don't care. Just too tired to."

He got out the Southern Pacific's money and handed it to him.

'It's a little short, but that's the bulk. I'll need a receipt."

"You'll get it."

Tutweiler came back out. He grinned at Raider. "That boy's sure got some nice things to say about you."

"He's two-thirds mouth and all asshole, him and his brother."

"I take it his daddy gave you conniption fits."

"And then some."

"Even dead he looks feisty as hell."

"That he was, the feistiest."

"Sure smells to high heaven. How'd you catch him?"

Raider sighed inwardly as he pictured his meal, his bottle, and his bed dissolving. He touched on the high points of the chase, skipping over his Shoshone disguise and Leroy Blodgett's arrival with the reinforcements, and he barely alluded to Sheriff Nat Abington and his role. He dwelt at length on Pickett.

"Tough as barbed wire. When we fought I hit and hit and couldn't hurt him, couldn't even dent his smirk. He was some shakes with a gun, too. Gutsy as they come. You could roll a rock over him he'd bounce back up swingin' like a windmill. Bust his bones, twist him outta all his sockets, kick him silly, bleed him white, even shoot him, he just wouldn't quit. He wore me down to a nub."

"Took a liking to him, didn't you?" said Tutweiler.

"Like I would a rattler."

"I mean it. Sounds to me like he gave you such a tussle you wound up admiring him."

"That's bullshit."

"Liking him," added Conklin. "Your eyes are getting all misty."

"You're nuts."

Tutweiler grinned. "Tears."

"No, no, that's a cold." In proof of which he promptly sneezed. "Jesus Christ, it is! It's him, he gave it to me. He had it, he musta sneezed me full in the face half a dozen times. I caught his damn cold!" Again he sneezed.

"That's a pretty good trick," said Conklin, "catching cold from a dead man."

"He wasn't dead when he did it, for Chrissakes! Gimme my receipt for the money, will ya? I gotta go."

Raider awoke in the middle of the night. He had eaten, gotten tolerably drunk, and crawled into bed. He awoke with a slight headache, and his mouth tasted like he'd been chewing on a sock, but otherwise he felt surprisingly good. Shedding the burden of the case, able to relax for the first time in days, helped. Someone was knocking at the door.

"Go 'way, I'm sleepin'."

"Mr. O'Toole?" asked a silky feminine voice.

He stiffened and looked down at his crotch covered by the sheet. "What d'ya want?" he asked politely, knowing full well the answer.

"What do you think?"

He got up, wrapped the sheet around him, and opened the door. Her flaming red hair was piled high on her head and liberally flecked with sequins. She was not pretty, but not jug ugly. He liked her smile. Her eyes were emerald green, suggesting that the color of her hair was natural. Her lips were full, glossed fire-engine red, and gleamed seductively. As his eyes descended her face in appraisal, arriving at her mouth, the tip of her tongue sneaked out between her lips invitingly. She was not young, perhaps even forty, but neither deeply lined nor drastically sagging in any place he could see at the moment. There was something familiar in her face. He couldn't immediately place it, but it was there. He thought back to DeLamar and Althea Mae, the last woman of inviting assets and easy virtue he had been close to. A regrettable encounter that. Still, it had been too long. He was overdue for a little friendly companionship, sweet-scented warmth, and the hauling of his ashes.

"May I come in?"

"I . . . ah, sure."

He stood aside, clutching the edge of the door with one hand, his sheet with the other.

"Mr. Longacre downstairs at the desk thought you might like a little company. Just come to town, have you?"

"This afternoon."

She was wearing a plum-colored velvet robe studded with sequins like those infesting her hair. The robe was trimmed with what looked like white chick down. He closed the door. She turned slowly and faced him. Her smile lit up the room. She reached for the front of her robe and drew the halves slowly apart. She was stark naked. He gulped. Her massive breasts rode high, their planes gleaming pink down to roseate nipples erect and as hard as nail heads. Her quim, boasting a generous thatch of red hair, beckoned invitingly. He swallowed. She dropped her robe. He choked.

"Like it?"

"Mmmmm, yeah, mmmm . . ."

She glided toward him, reached forth, and removed his sheet

"My my, what have we here?" Again he swallowed. "May I?"

She sank to her knees. Her tongue felt warm, verging on hot. She began beating restlessly about his cock, raising and firming it, laving it from his jewels upward, then back down, nipping his balls lightly, playfully, then seizing his erection and slowly burying it down her throat. He groaned and began to back toward the bed, bringing her hot mouth with him, sitting slowly, carefully, lest he sever the connection.

She began to suck, driving her face hard against his root, engorging him, devouring him, sucking, sucking, gently drawing the life from him, spreading weakness throughout his body, languor taking over, melting him, reducing his every limb, every bone, shrinking him until he was no longer a man, but a blob of quivering flesh poised at the root end of his cock with all his strength and energy thrust forward into it. Sucked and sucked and sucked, filling his balls, steeling them, unlocking them, freeing his ejaculation, sending it hurtling upward and out, thrashing, drenching her throat.

And still she sucked, on and on without losing a beat. His erection softened, he became limper and limper, but she took no notice, sucking rhythmically, easily, seemingly intent on freeing his cock from his crotch as gently as she could to swallow it. He began to harden again. Harder. Harder. Throbbing, pulsating, he came again, splattering her mouth.

He lay back on the bed, groaning. Every bone in his body but one had dissolved. She was now in full command. A third time she sucked him hard, kissed his head in signal that it was ready, and positioning herself directly over, began assaulting her cunt with his head, rubbing it gently at first, then more rigorously. He was panting, sweating, reveling in her glorious abuse. Suddenly she stopped.

"What's the matter?" he blurted.

"What must you think of me?'

"Huh?"

"That I'm no lady, that's for certain sure. Here I barge in on you, and start in playing and I completely forgot to introduce myself. You're John."

"Yeah, yeah."

"I'm Rosie. Rose."

"Yeah, good."

"Guess what?"

"What? What?"

"You'll never guess. My name, Rose, is not just my first name, it's my initials too. I'll bet you've never met anybody whose first name is their initials too. Have you? Have you?" .

"No."

"Rose is Rose and also stands for Rose o' Sharon Elsie. R-o-s-e. Get it? Rose is Rose o' Sharon Elsie."

He gasped. "Rose—"

"—O' Sharon Elsie."

"Pick—"

"—Pickett, right." She stiffened and stared. "How did you know?"

"Just . . . guessed."

"That's my last name. It is. How could you 'just guess' my last name? What's happening? What's the matter, you're all of a sudden getting soft as a grape. Look, it's limp. It's pitiful. Shot to hell."

"I'm sorry."

"What do you mean, 'sorry'? I practically eat you to death, climb on, it's hard as a mill file, I'm hot as a pistol ready to fuck, and you—"

"I said I'm sorry, didn't I? What the hell you want from me, you think I'm made o' iron? I'm human, you know. Three hard-ons in six minutes is one helluva lot. Whatta ya think, I can just keep gettin' harder and harder all night long? Gimme a break, willya?"

"I'll give ya a break! I'll give ya a break!"

She was suddenly furious. Off she jumped. She snatched up her robe and pulled it on. "What are you, a fairy? Hard as a rock, soft as an egg in the wink of an eye? You must be!"

"Oh, bullshit!"

"Give me five dollars."

"Five?"

"That's what I said. Pay up, Mr. Soft."

"I'll give ya two."

"Four!"

"Two and two bits."

"Give, cheapskate."

He paid her. She flew out the door, impaling him with her glare, chiding him for his failure, slamming the door. He locked it and sat down on the bed, continuing captive of his astonishment.

"Jesus, if she only knew. If she did she'da yanked it off me and tossed it out the window. Of all the crazy . . . Wait'll I tell Weatherbee." He saw his amazement reflected in the mirror above the washbasin. "What are you talkin' about? You don't tell him a damn thing. You don't tell anybody. It didn't happen, not really. It was all a bad dream. It was those greasy cottage fries and the onions.

"Rose o' Sharon Elsie Pickett. Holy Hannah!"

CHAPTER NINETEEN

He tried his best to thrust Rose o' Sharon Elsie out of his mind the next morning, but it wasn't easy. He was still slightly stunned by the episode. It was like Ira was reaching out of the grave to get his goat. He checked with Sheriff Conklin to make sure Caleb was still locked up. In Doc's stead he would have to wire the agency and bring the chief up to date. It wasn't an obligation he looked forward to with any great relish, but there was no way to avoid it. Losing twelve operatives on a single assignment had to be a record, he thought, as he stood at the counter in the Western Union office laboriously comprising his message. Try as he might there was no way to soften the news. The chief would probably have a stroke, and losing his pet operative, his "third son," as Doc once referred to Blodgett, would be the capper. He wouldn't be surprised if he and Doc were ordered to catch the first train to Chicago to report in person to the main office and undergo a grilling calculated to roast them to a turn.

"Stay where you are, Doc, as long as you like. You're our excuse for stickin' round."

He sent his report collect. He stood outside the office, leaning against the overhang post, mulling over the events of the past few days, trying with limited success to assemble them in proper order, but the whole thing was such a jumble it was impossible. Plunged into thought, he failed to notice his caller of the previous night approaching until she was little more than an arm's length away. At the sound of her step he lifted his head and his face out of shadow. Her eyes landed and began drilling. She didn't speak, didn't have to. Her expression said it all. He was the world's greatest bedroom failure: Mr. Soft, the collapsible client. He might as well have been dirt or something fouler beneath her slipper-shod foot from the look she gave him. One word only passed her lips as she passed him, with even the rustling of her skirts sounding critical.

"Pathetic."

On she sailed. He shuddered slightly, as if to rid himself of the recollection of the dismal ending to the night before. He hoped he wouldn't have to hang around for Caleb's trial. She'd be there, no question. When she found out his connection to her family and what had happened to Ira and his eldest she'd probably come after him with a shotgun.

Then and there he vowed that it would be in the best interests of his continued good health if he saddled up and rode back to Murphy. He'd be foolish to stick around for Ira and Jace's funerals. She'd hear, she'd show up, she'd fire questions at everybody, she'd find out about his role. Yes, a shotgun. Either that or a pitchfork.

He could keep Doc company until he was back on his feet.

"That's what I'll do. Loaf round the rest o' the day, make sure Conklin's all squared away with the kid and doesn't need me for anything, have myself a couple more good meals, and take off first thing tomorrow."

MESSAGE RECEIVED STOP A PITY YOU WERE UNABLE TO PREVENT WHOLESALE SLAUGHTER YOUR FELLOW

OPERATIVES STOP FIND YOUR SURVIVAL EXTRAORDI-
NARY IN LIGHT OF WHAT HAPPENED TO OTHERS STOP
WERE YOU DIRECTLY INVOLVED STOP EQUALLY DIS-
TRESSING IS YOUR NEWS RE GANG STOP BRINGING
BACK SON OF LEADER ONLY DOES NOT EXACTLY
SMACK OF TRIUMPHAL RETURN STOP ASSUME YOU DID
BEST YOU COULD HOWEVER CANNOT HELP NOTING IT
WAS NONE TOO GOOD IN THIS INSTANCE STOP UNDER
CIRCUMSTANCES REQUIRE CONSIDERABLY MORE
THAN STANDARD CASE JOURNAL REPORT STOP YOUR
PRESENCE REQUIRED ASAP STOP TRUST WEATHERBEE
ON MEND STOP IN VIEW HIS CONDITION HE NEED NOT
APPEAR STOP YOU NEED NOT WAIT FOR HIS RECOVERY
ENABLING TO DO SO STOP LOOK FORWARD TO SEEING
YOU STOP IF YOU CONTACT WEATHERBEE CONVEY MY
HEARTFELT HOPE FOR HIS SPEEDY RECOVERY STOP HIS
COURAGE COOPERATION AND CONSCIENTIOUSNESS
ARE AS ALWAYS TO HIS EVERLASTING CREDIT STOP
OTHER OPERATIVES WOULD DO WELL TO EMULATE HIS
SHINING EXAMPLE

AP

"Bullshit!"

"I beg your pardon," said the clerk, frowning.

"Not you, him. Never mind. Why'd you have to roust
me outta my bed crack o' dawn just for this bullshit?"

The clerk's eyes narrowed and his small jaw thrust forward belligerently. "I thought it might be important. Pardon my error. That'll be a dollar seventy."

"For what?"

"It was sent collect."

"Like hell!"

"It was sent collect."

He showed him the receipt. Raider continued grumbling
long after he paid him and left, leaving Allan Pinkerton's
response to his telegram in a crumpled ball on the wooden
sidewalk out front.

"I never got it, A.P. Never knew you sent one, bein' as I

already left town. So there's no way in the world I could know you want me shaggin' back there so's you can haul me on the carpet and push your pins into me. Murphy, Doc, here I come."

"We really botched this one, didn't we?" said Doc morosely.

He was able to sit propped up by two pillows. His pajama tops were open to reveal a large bandage swathing his chest. His color was slowly coming back. He talked in between sips of chicken broth fed him by his partner.

"Bullshit! We got Ira, didn't we? I did. Woulda had both his brats too with a little luck. But you know me and luck, we see each other we run and hide."

"I understand they found two bodies in the Owyhees in a ravine up above the pocket where the shack was located."

"That'd be Hudlin and McColl."

"I figured. That's what I told the reporters."

"Reporters?"

"A small army of them showed up day before yesterday to interview me."

"What bullshit. Besides, what the hell do you know 'bout the case, 'bout Ira and his kids? You and Leroy were all wrapped up with the lynchin'. I did all the work, for Chrissakes."

"I know, but I couldn't tell them much about your taking him in and all. I didn't know. There was no way of knowing you'd even reach Elko."

"Bullshit! You got some low 'pinion o' my balls, savvy, and follow-through, you have. Thanks a lot."

"I didn't down you to them."

"You didn't up me neither. Forget it. Who cares 'bout reporters and newspapers anyhow. What's with the photographer's wife? How's she doin'?"

"As well as can be expected. She comes to see me every day." He nodded toward a bouquet of daisies in a slender vase on the windowsill. "What'll they do with Caleb?"

"What d'ya think? He was in on Aaron Cobble's

murder, in on the holdup. If they don't give him life they'll hang him. When are you gonna get outta this dump?"

"It'll be at least one more week, and even then I'll have to bend Dr. Von Zell's arm to let me put my pants on. Did you remember to wire Chicago?"

"Yeah, yeah."

"And?"

"And what?"

"Did you get an answer?"

"Yeah."

"What did the chief say? Was he terribly upset? He must have been. Where's the telegram?"

Raider made a pretense of going through his pockets. "I musta mislaid it."

"Was it singed around the edges?"

"Naw."

"I got one myself. It's under that glass on the stand. Don't you want to read it?"

"If that's what it takes to shut you up about it."

SINCERE WISHES FROM ALL OF US FOR YOUR SPEEDY RECOVERY STOP YOUR EXEMPLARY CONDUCT THROUGHOUT THIS MOST TRAGIC AFFAIR BROUGHT TO OUR ATTENTION BY WIRE SERVICE STORIES STOP A PITY YOUR PARTNER COULDNT HAVE BEEN MORE HELPFUL STOP IN VIEW OF YOUR SPLENDID SERVICE TO THE AGENCY IN RECOGNITION OF YOUR DILIGENCE AND DEVOTION TO DUTY I AM TODAY PUTTING THROUGH A SIZABLE RAISE IN SALARY FOR YOU STOP HOPEFULLY IT WILL SERVE AS INCENTIVE TO OTHER OPERATIVES STOP CONGRATULATIONS

"Bullshit!"

"Rade . . ."

"Bullshit!"

"Will you quiet down. If I thought it was going to upset

you this much I wouldn't have asked you to read it."

"Not much."

"What are you doing? Where are you going?"

"I'm goin' out to tie one on, then I'm gonna sleep it off, then I'm gonna get up and write my letter o' resignation."

"Of course."

"I mean it, Doc. I've had it up to here. I can't take any more."

Continuing to rant and ramble, he stormed out the door, but not before crumpling Doc's telegram and throwing it in what remained of his chicken broth.

JAKE LOGAN

___ 07567-2	**SLOCUM'S PRIDE**	$2.50
___ 07382-3	**SLOCUM AND THE GUN-RUNNERS**	$2.50
___ 08382-9	**SLOCUM IN DEADWOOD**	$2.50
___ 10442-7	**VIGILANTE JUSTICE**	$2.75
___ 10443-5	**JAILBREAK MOON**	$2.75
___ 10444-3	**MESCALERO DAWN**	$2.75
___ 08539-6	**DENVER GOLD**	$2.50
___ 08742-5	**SLOCUM AND THE HORSE THIEVES**	$2.50
___ 08773-5	**SLOCUM AND THE NOOSE OF HELL**	$2.50
___ 08791-3	**CHEYENNE BLOODBATH**	$2.50
___ 09088-4	**THE BLACKMAIL EXPRESS**	$2.50
___ 09111-2	**SLOCUM AND THE SILVER RANCH FIGHT**	$2.50
___ 09299-2	**SLOCUM AND THE LONG WAGON TRAIN**	$2.50
___ 09212-7	**SLOCUM AND THE DEADLY FEUD**	$2.50
___ 09342-5	**RAWHIDE JUSTICE**	$2.50
___ 09395-6	**SLOCUM AND THE INDIAN GHOST**	$2.50
___ 09479-0	**SEVEN GRAVES TO LAREDO**	$2.50
___ 09567-3	**SLOCUM AND THE ARIZONA COWBOYS**	$2.50
___ 09647-5	**SIXGUN CEMETERY**	$2.75
___ 09712-9	**SLOCUM'S DEADLY GAME**	$2.75
___ 09896-6	**HELL'S FURY**	$2.75
___ 10016-2	**HIGH, WIDE AND DEADLY**	$2.75

Talons of the Eagle